A
FASHION
TO KILL

A
FASHION
TO KILL

A MYSTERY NOVEL

MICKEY WYTE

A FASHION TO KILL
Copyright © 2012 Mickey Wyte

Cover Design by www.jeroentenberge.com
eBook Design & Formatting by the eBook Artisans

For Janet, My Muse

And To
Sherry and Jen
Thanks for Everything!

The skin hardens to form a scar tissue
protecting the once raw wound.

Years later, when touched in a certain way,
all the pain will return.

ONE

A CAMERA FLASHED BEHIND ME. She was dead. Her body lay at my feet. The back of her long, black satin skirt drawn up, revealing a glimpse of her buttocks and the hint of a sheer pink thong. The front of the skirt fanned out away from her legs, as if an autumn breeze had crossed the room just before she was found. She never wore stockings. She didn't need to. Her legs were firm and muscular. Like a dancer's legs. She had loved to dance. From one leg, slightly bent at the knee, a black, stiletto-heeled Prada shoe hung off a tanned foot, exposing a high, sensuous white arch. The other leg extended straight out, with its long tapered shoe pointing like a spear toward the door.

She was nearly five feet nine. Five feet eight and three-quarters, to be exact. She had modeled for a while in high school. Gave it up because forced starving was not her thing. She loved life too much. Her black bra had been removed and lay inches from the glossy red fingernails of her outstretched hand. A ruby nipple peeked from beneath a black silk blouse. Her hair was cut in a 1920's flapper style. The girl loved everything about the Roaring Twenties. I would not have noticed the small puncture at the base of her neck were it not for the crimson pool of blood coagulating on the cold white tile floor.

When the camera flashed again I knew how the headline, sprawled across the front page of the *New York Journal*, would read:

FASHION KILLER ICE-PICKS SEXY 4TH VICTIM!

This is what detectives wearing thin, milky-white latex gloves, stretched across their thick, street-hardened hands, stood over. This is what the team of coroners, who had just arrived, was about to inspect. To touch. To probe. To cart off to the morgue. This is what they saw, and what the city of neon and concrete would see. I saw something different.

I saw alternating flashes of a child and of a woman. I saw the muscular legs; I saw the puff of baby-fat they had once possessed. I saw the thong; I saw Pampers. I saw dyed black hair; I saw the half-dozen shades she had colored her natural mouse-brown she had hated so much. What I saw lying on that bathroom floor, in a suite in one of the city's trendiest boutique hotels, was my sister's kid. It was my name, Jack Centaur, that the detectives had found written on the emergency card in her purse. It was my cell phone that had rung while I ate a late dinner alone at my usual table at Elaine's.

I was the only father she'd ever known. And now she was dead, and I had to accept it. And I knew now, too, that I was going to be the one who would open a door and face her mother.

I stood, staring down at this woman-child dead at my feet, and a sudden rush of heat pervaded my insides. Bile retched up my esophagus. I swallowed hard to hold down the sour, burning vomit.

And in that instant, I knew how all the fathers, and how all the mothers, had felt when the picture they saw sprawled on the front page was *their* kid.

And I knew one more thing. I knew The Fashion Killer must pay, and pay big, for the death of my niece, Candice Nolen, and the three other innocent victims.

It was in that instant, gagging on the rancid, vile taste of murder, that I anointed myself the collector of the debt.

TWO

I WOKE AT DAWN. I hadn't shaved since the funeral. My five-o'clock shadow, fertilized for three straight days by a steady flow of Chivas Regal, had grown into the salt-speckled beard of an old man. The sudden ringing of the forgotten alarm clock pierced my head like a Con Edison drill. As I turned from the mirror, my shaky hand lost grip of the toothbrush. It fell down into the toilet bowl. My heart was down there somewhere too.

I stuck my hand into the commode, retrieved the toothbrush and tossed it into the bathroom trash basket, showered and shaved.

I STUDIED THE wall of bespoke 42 regulars in my dressing closest. I pulled down a navy-blue three-button pinstripe. The label read: Gieves and Hawke, No. 1 Savile Row, London.

I eyed the dozens of dress shirts hanging along the far wall. All 16¾ inch spread collars. All Sea Isle cotton, custom-made for me in Ireland. All lightly starched, never folded. I chose a pale blue one.

I started the electric tie rack. A hundred silk neckties rotated past my eyes. I stopped the rack on a charcoal gray with thin red diagonal stripes that I had purchased in Paris. The stripes matched the bloodshot veins in the whites of my eyes.

I pulled open one of the three sock drawers and removed a folded pair of navy cashmere mid-calves.

My closet was like a shoe store specializing in only one size: four wide shelves of ten double-E. I picked up a pair of sturdy cordovan oxford wingtips, handmade by Church's of London. I was now ready to do business.

FREDDY CAUGHT SIGHT of his favorite tenant crossing the lobby and was quick to hold open the glass door for me. He tapped the brim of his doorman's cap, smiling. "Morning, Mr. Centaur."

Thirty years at his post, Freddy knew that "morning" was all he should say today. He'd save his chatter concerning the ordeal of the city's sporting teams for another day.

"Cab, Freddy."

"Sure thing, Mr. Centaur," Freddy said, rushing to the curb.

Freddy leaned into Fifth Avenue, casting his arm out like a seasoned fisherman into a sea of yellow taxicabs, all pushing to make the traffic light at the corner of West Eighth Street before it turned red. He hooked a cab before I reached the curb. Now Freddy held open yet another door for his favorite tenant.

I slipped two crisp, folded hundred-dollar bills into Freddy's palm. It was the first of the month and I always paid up front for the service I expected.

Freddy tugged a "Thank You" from the brim of his cap with his left hand. His right hand discreetly slipped the two hundred down deep into his jacket pocket.

I slid across the back seat of the cab, saying, "2087 Montague Street."

In the rearview mirror I caught the driver's grimace. Cabbies hate leaving Manhattan during the morning rush, afraid they'll be driving back empty. I checked the hack license posted on the dashboard and said, "Ivan, you get me to Brooklyn in a hurry and it's double the meter."

The cab screeched from the curb, making the light at the corner just as the caution yellow turned to red. Caution wasn't on my agenda any longer. I'd been playing the sedentary good guy for too many years. Since Candice's murder, memories I long ago buried beneath

the scar tissue of time had surfaced in me like the forgotten pain of
an old wound.

The Russian maneuvered through the downtown traffic like a
Cossack on a vodka run. We hit the ramp of the Brooklyn Bridge
in nothing flat.

Brooklyn is called the City of Churches, and the Brooklyn Bridge
is its cathedral runway, with a thousand steel spires glistening in the
sunlight like an angel's harp. As the cab passed between the first pair
of the bridge's weathered gothic stone towers, I cocked my head to
the right. The crisp September sun was reflecting gold off the glass
and steel of the Financial District. Downriver I saw a crowded ferry
disembarking its last group of rush hour commuters from the tip of
Staten Island to the granite rock of Manhattan Island. Once on the
pier, this mass of office workers would disperse like columns of army
ants, racing to padded cubicles to settle in for the grind of another
eight-hour shift.

I turned, now facing forward, staring blankly ahead as the taxi
descended the Brooklyn side of the Bridge, wondering who was now
filling Candice's cubicle.

Straight out of high school she went to work for me at Smoothe
Press. That was, until the morning she came into my office announcing she didn't want a future as the boss's niece. Said she wanted to
make it on her own. So she quit working for her uncle and began
paralegal classes at John Jay.

The kid did okay; landed a position as a legal assistant to
Michael Lawson. Michael was head of Legal Affairs, as Michael's
father, Bradford, liked to call the two-person department at Lawson
Worldwide. Bradford Lawson was well known for exaggerations.

Twenty-three, still living at home with her mother, she'd make
it to her cubicle each morning on the number 2 train from Court
Street Station in Brooklyn to the Fourteenth Street-Union Square
Station in Manhattan. Inside the cab I closed my eyes, imagining
my niece hurrying the eight blocks from Union Square to Lawson
Worldwide, making a quick stop to pick up her breakfast—bagel and
coffee, maybe—at Dean and Deluca on the way.

Damn, she had everything going for her. The brains, the beauty. And the balls!

Now the cab was off the bridge and rumbling over one of the few remaining cobblestone streets in Brooklyn, taking me back to a time etched in my mind as if it were yesterday, when horse-drawn wagons carried fresh produce from the waterfront to the pushcarts along Fulton Street. A time when we'd have held up our stickball game to allow these wagons to pass. Sometimes a kid would hitch a ride to the corner by hanging from the back of the wagon, the driver never the wiser, then the kid would jump off and run back to our game to take his turn at bat. When was the last time I'd seen any kids playing stickball? Now the only stickball being played in the city was by out-of-shape middle-aged men like myself, with weak legs and more road behind them than ahead, who seriously believed they could still hit a pink Spaldeen ball for a two-sewers home run.

"Montague Street," the Russian grunted, snapping me back to the present.

THREE

STOOD AT THE CURB, looking up at the four-story brownstone where my sister Betty lived on the second floor. When we were kids we lived in that same second-floor apartment with our parents. Our parents had been longtime renters of Mr. and Mrs. Weiner, even after the Weiner family, what was left of it, moved away. Now I owned the place. I rented the first floor to a yuppie couple with a two-year-old son. A lesbian couple rented the third floor. The fourth floor? Well, the fourth floor had its purpose.

I climbed the six wide steps to the top of the stoop and stood now facing the solid oak front door. I reached out with my left hand to the side panel and pressed the black button next to Nolen—I only used my passkey the times when I needed to. A moment of silence, then the front door lock buzzed. I inhaled the last bit of the street air into my lungs for courage and pushed the oak door open.

I climbed the thirteen steps to the second floor. When I reached the top of the staircase, Betty was standing beneath the transom of her apartment door.

Betty was born eight years after me. That morning, in the dim light of the second floor landing, she looked tens years older than me.

"Three days," she whispered, "Not even a phone call," and turned away, walking into the apartment.

I stepped into the parlor. "Betts," I said, her back to me as she crept on into the living room. "I couldn't come back so soon." I let the sentence drift silent, knowing my sister understood the words left unsaid, so soon after throwing a shovel full of dark earth into a six-foot-deep hole next to the headstone of Edward Nolen, *a union man with a promised future robbed by a faulty scaffold*, and praying that father and daughter would finally have their time together.

Betty huddled on the couch, clutching a throw pillow. The blue-and-orange Mets sweats she had on looked slept in. Disheveled newspapers lay everywhere.

I cleared a place next to my sister and gently touched her shoulders. She looked up from the pillow. There was no venom in her eyes, only hurt.

She leaned into me. I felt her sobs against my chest. She reached a hand up to touch my face. I turned my head so she could not feel the tears running down my cheeks.

We sat for a while without speaking, wondering what was next for us.

"I know you Jackie," my sister finally said, pulling her head away from my chest. "You've got to let the police handle things."

My jaw tightened at the mention of the police. Those buried memories were surfacing again.

"Jackie, it was a long time ago. The police *have* changed," she emphasized, clutching my hand, her fingers, cold and clammy against my skin. "Promise me, you'll let the police do their job."

Even if I wanted to lie, I couldn't get away with it. My sister knew me better than anyone knew me. But she didn't know all of me. Or all I was capable of doing.

"I'm going to meet with the detective working the case. I promise you, I'll hear him out." And that was all the truth I could give my sister.

Betty rose from the couch. "You want some tea?"

I had stopped drinking coffee around the time I turned fifty. Acid heartburn.

"Thanks," I said, getting up to kiss her cheek.

Betty went into the kitchen and I straightened up the mess in the living room. Picking up a week-old copy of *The New York Journal* off the coffee table, I could not help looking once more at the front-page picture of Candice's body. I had stared at that picture a thousand times during the three days and three nights I tried drowning myself in a sea of scotch. But those three blurred days of being a horse's ass were behind me. My head was clear now. My wits sharp.

And now I had a cop to see.

FOUR

SQUEEZED BETWEEN A MOAT of blue-and-white patrol cars wedged vertically into the curb of West Twenty-Second Street, and walked through the gothic archway entrance of the 33rd Precinct.

Once inside, a cacophony of chaotic voices and a rushing current of blue uniforms assaulted me. Not much had changed in the thirty-five years since I'd last entered a police precinct. Only this time, when I looked up at the uniformed sergeant perched like a centurion behind the elevated front desk, I wasn't intimidated.

"Tell Detective Dent Mr. Centaur is here."

"He expectin' you?"

"Yeah."

"Wa for?"

"Ask him."

The sergeant leaned over the desk. "Hey, what'd a you a some kind of wise-ass or somethin'?"

I didn't reply. Just kept staring straight up at his fat, red face.

The sergeant grimaced, picking up the desk phone. "Someone called Centaur down here asking for you." The sergeant listened, then, nodding to a narrow staircase off to his left, he grunted at me, "Second floor."

"You don't remember me, do you?" Detective Dent said, leading me to a city issued steel desk at the back of the dingy Second Floor Squad Room.

"You think I have Alzheimer's or something? Can't remember the guy who asked me to identify my dead niece?"

"Sorry. No. Mr. Centaur," Dent backed off. Maybe his streetwise instincts were telling him I had something against cops. "But, we have met before. Before the unfortunate circumstance that brought us together last week."

I scanned my gray matter for a clue as to where and when I would have crossed paths with this man who held an uncanny resemblance to a young Sidney Poitier.

"P-A-L," Dent hinted.

"P-A-L? When the hell—" Then I recalled the Police Athletic League fundraiser I had been roped into attending. "Yeah, yeah," I said. "What was it? About a year ago?"

Dent smiled. "More like three."

"Whew, three years ago! You sure?" I grimaced, feeling the years slipping by as fast as months.

Dent grinned. "Yep. We even shot a few baskets in the gym with some of the kids."

"That's right. Sure. But you weren't so hot from the foul line. I remember the kids were busting your chops real good."

"If you think my foul shots are something bad," Dent laughed, "my wife won't let me go near a dance floor."

"Well, I'm sure your real talent is finding killers," I said, getting back to the present.

"Please, sit down," Dent said.

I slid a straight-back steel chair away from the front of the desk and sat down. Dent walked behind the desk and sat in a duplicate of my chair, facing me, and sighed. "To be honest with you, Mr. Centaur, this case is going nowhere."

Behind the detective, a coat hanger hung from a nail banged into a dingy gray wall. Around the nail the wall was chipped, revealing layers of paint like the time rings of an ancient tree. I glimpsed at the clean and pressed black suit jacket hanging on the coat hanger. Dent dressed well—for a cop. Though I figured the suit for a definite Men's Wearhouse rack job.

"That's not what I want you to be telling me," I said. "What I want you to be telling me is that you're about to close in on the bastard. That you've got a suspect right this minute being grilled under a hot light in some cold, damp room, down in the basement here. That you've got the bastard sweating beads, and just about five seconds away from confessing before two burly beasts, stuffed into jelly-stained white shirts, beat the hell out him. That's what I want you to be telling me, Detective Dent. Not some bullshit that the case is going nowhere."

Dent leaned back in his chair, clasping his big hands behind his head, studying the man sitting across from him. After a long minute, leaning forwarded again, pulling his hands away from the back of his head, placing them down on the steel desk and interlocking his manicured fingers, he said, "I've been on this case since the first murder, Mr. Centaur. I've seen how hard it is for the victim's family. Look, right now you'd just love to get your hands around someone's neck. But it ain't going to happen. There's no one in custody. No one I could give up to you even if I wanted to."

Now Dent pulled a small spiral notepad from the breast pocket of his starched white shirt. "I need to ask you a few questions about your niece," he said, flipping through the pad's dog-eared pages.

"Go ahead," I said, turning in the stiff chair, crossing my legs.

"Boyfriend?"

"No."

"Any in the past that might have broken off badly?"

"Not that I know of."

"Drug use?"

"No!"

"Candice do the club scene a lot?"

"As much as any kid her age, I guess."

Dent checked off each answer in the pad in a manner seeming too routine. As if he were priming me for some kind of bombshell.

"Any—"

"Come on, Detective," I snapped. "Let's get to the point. What's the angle here? My niece is this monster's fourth victim. What do they all have in common? That's what you're searching for. Right?"

"Right," Dent replied, and then continued his questioning as if the man sitting across from him had never spoken.

"Any friends you didn't approve of?"

"Detective." I felt an ache in my temples, the Chivas headache was returning. "Candice didn't report to me."

Dent looked up from the notepad. "How about a girlfriend? She have any ex-lovers who might have been upset with her?"

If this was Dent's bombshell then its fuse was wet.

"As far as I know, she's never had a relationship so awful that someone would want to kill her over a breakup." I shifted my weight in the steel chair. "Detective, you sound like a guy desperate to grasp at any straw in the wind. How about you do some talking. Tell me what you've got so far. Damn it, I've got a right to know. Haven't I? It's my niece who's dead!"

Dent flipped his pad closed, tossing it onto the desk. "You want to know what I've got just read the tabloids, they seem to know it all. I've got four dead women. All in their twenties, all lesbians, all volunteering as fashion models for Young Metropolitans League charity galas, all with a single puncture going up into the base of their brain, and all making the front page of the *Journal* look like a photo shoot for *Harper's Bazaar*. That's what I've got, Mr. Centaur."

"And no leads!" I said, uncrossing my legs, leaning forward, my forearms now pressing hard against the edge of the detective's sparse desk. "Not even one?"

"Mr. Centaur, I remember *you* at the foul line at the P.A.L. fundraiser. I remember a big guy, your business partner, right? Yeah, your partner. A guy named Smoothe. He was egging you on, busting your chops. Called it luck when you finally made a shot from the line. Said he would donate a hundred bucks for every foul shot you made until you missed. Said he wasn't worried, it wasn't going to cost him much. You zoned in on that hoop, and it cost him a grand. And don't think I don't know that now you're trying to zone in on the bum who killed your niece. But I'm afraid it's my official duty to tell you to back off and let me do my job."

"Back off, my ass," I said, now half-standing up from that goddamned stiff chair. "Someone has to dive in here because I can see that you guys have ungotz."

"What are you going to do, Mr. Centaur, stalk this city like you were searching for snipers in Nam?"

"What the hell'd you do, run a background check on me? Like I'm some kind of criminal. Isn't there a law about running background checks without just cause?"

"You ever Google yourself, Mr. Centaur?"

"Nah," I said, sitting back down in the chair. "I heard it could make a guy go blind."

"You ought to try it. Be surprised at what comes up."

"Surprise me," I grunted.

Dent picked up his notepad again, flipped through a few more pages, found what he was looking for and read out loud:

"February 12, 1969, Specialist 4th class Jack Centaur, 4th Infantry Division. Platoon is pinned down under sniper fire. Six U.S. soldiers have been hit. Specialist Centaur low-crawls through the bush until he sees where the shots are coming from. Then Specialist Centaur takes out three snipers. A single shot at a time." Dent looked up from the pad. "Got you the Congressional Medal of Honor."

I shrugged. "Got me one day closer to making it home."

"Got a platoon full of soldiers a day closer, too."

"I didn't do it for them."

"That's not what Congress said." Dent didn't look at his notepad this time; he knew what it read. And so did I. *"Specialist Jack Centaur demonstrated unselfish courage under fire."*

"Congress has been known to make mistakes," I said.

"Not when it comes to the Medal of Honor."

"Look, we're not here to discuss my past. We're here to discuss the present. So let's get down to how you're going to earn your pay."

"Mr. Centaur, there are rules, procedures, for apprehending a criminal. Rules I'm bound by my oath to follow."

"Rules that can hold you back from getting results."

Dent leaned forward. Now *his* forearms were pressed against the edge of the desk. "I will not break the rules."

"Of course not," I said. "Then, you'd be no better than the criminal you're chasing."

"Riiight." The word slid from the detective's lips like a slow barge pushing its way up the Hudson River.

"Detective, I'm not a cop. I don't give a shit about rules or procedures or whatever the hell you want to call these things that cripple you from finding the bad guys. I don't even really give a shit now what clues you might have. All I need are people—people I can push my way through until someone slips up. As they always do. The dishonest ones. And then I'll collect what's owed to me."

"You think you can muscle your way through all of New York City?"

"Maybe if you bent, no lets say—curved—a rule just little to help me narrow down the field."

Dent cocked his head, looking now even more like Sidney Poitier. I figured the man was about to give something up. Some compass point for me to follow. Instead he stood up.

"Thank you for coming in, Mr. Centaur," he said, offering his business card.

I took the card.

Now offering his hand, Dent said, "And again, please allow me to offer my condolences, and my promise to you and Mrs. Nolen that the perpetrator will be apprehended."

It was a businessman's habit, I guess. Maybe. Or perhaps it was just the right thing to do. Whatever. But I found myself gripping the detective's offered hand. He had a firm handshake. Not like a politician's or a conman's flesh-pressing firm handshake. Dent's felt like the honest handshake of a man I would usually lean towards trusting.

But Dent was still a cop. And I wasn't going to trust him. Not yet.

FIVE

"Sɪxᴛɪᴇᴛʜ ᴀɴᴅ Fɪғᴛʜ Aᴠᴇɴᴜᴇ," I told the cabbie.

I didn't take Dent for a dumb cop. I figured he was sharp enough to know that if he wanted to get the lowdown on the society set, he would need someone on the inside. Someone who can go where they don't allow blue collars to go. I told myself he'd come around soon enough. He was in a bad spot.

Well, I knew my way around the society set all right. I had the money—not old-line money, but money good enough to buy my way in. And I knew their minds. The society rich. Smoothe Press printed the gratuitous programs for most of the high-ticket charity banquets in the city where the rich showcased their philanthropic consciences.

Now it was time for me to do a little research of my own. Fill my own little notebook of questions.

I entered through the East Sixtieth Street gate of the limestone building that was home to The New York Heritage Club. Inside, the tall oak-paneled walls, the gold paint of the vaulted ceiling, and the Italian marble floor all hinted of a time when New York City had been at its grandest. A time when the nouveau riche still had roots in the old world, a world where a respect for history was considered an intellectual hallmark of the wealthy. Even with all their carpetbagger faults, men like Carnegie, Frisk and Mellon still had had enough decency, and good taste, to pay homage to the city that allowed them their fortunes by erecting monumental structures of strong stone that would stand the test of time. Men like Bradford Lawson built hyperbolized structures of glass that glittered with the family brand.

It was 3 PM. I hadn't had a thing in my stomach all day except the pallid cup of Lipton bag tea Betty had given me. Afternoon Tea was being served in the third floor member's lounge of the New York Heritage Club.

A waiter dressed in a red cadet jacket with six brass buttons, each emblazoned with the initials NYHC, set a sterling silver teapot and a three-tiered tray of finger sandwiches, scones and petite pastries down on the mahogany table next to the tall back leather chair where I now sat. I glanced at my Patek Philippe. It read 3:25 PM. I let the pot of Assam steep while I wolfed down the finger sandwiches. I glanced again at my timepiece; exactly seven minutes had passed. The tea would be perfect now.

I placed the silver tea strainer across the thin rim of the white bone-china cup that had the same NYHC initials emblazoned in Wedgwood blue on its side. I lifted the teapot and poured the liquid through the silver strainer. It was piping hot, and as dark as black coffee.

At 3:50 PM I signed the club chit, and left the members' lounge for the first floor library.

The library was the reason I had joined the club. The long mahogany tables, and the sweet fragrance of the books lining the walls, rivaled the more famed Grand Reading Room of the New York Public Library on Fifth Avenue, built a full ten years after the room where I now sat in front of a computer screen with the Google home page awaiting my input.

I have the mind of a financial analyst, a compulsive mind of minute details waiting like digital pixels to form an image. I was trained to focus on one line, one item, one dollar at a time when searching a company's books. Eventually, even in the most devious of enterprises, where the sharpest minds schemed, someone hid an item in the wrong column. It's was my job to catch it. And I always did. That's why Andy made me his partner.

What I knew of the murders was only through skimming the tabloid pages, and the quick "Shocking Details at Eleven" television blurbs. The only conversations on the subject I had had were the what-kind-of-nut-would-do-something-like-this office-talk with Andy. And, the stop-worrying-nothing-is-going-to-happen-to-Candice kind with Betty.

I two-fingered "Fashion Killer" on the keyboard and Googled up fifteen pages of reference, including several scam sites selling memorial T-shirts. Most references were to blogs. I hit on a couple and quickly saw they were run by idiots wanting to connect the killings to everything from a CIA conspiracy to Lee Harvey Oswald, purported to be still alive and getting back at his mother by killing young women in New York City.

I decided to go to the website of *The New York Journal*. It seemed it was the rag getting the most mileage and, I'd bet, the most revenues out of reporting the story than any of the city's three other newspapers.

Sure enough, the *Journal* had archived all the articles, accompanied by a gory front-page photograph of each victim.

I attempted to focus on the pictures and read the copy and avoid being distracted by the various pop-up ads.

Click.

FEBRUARY 25, 2006
MODEL SLAIN IN CHELSEA APARTMENT

Dana Cummings, 22, body was found early this morning in her apartment on West 16th Street.

Ms. Cummings, last seen at The Mocha Shoppe, when not pursuing her high fashion modeling career, worked there as a waitress, hashing out food and drinks to the gaggle of editors, agents, photographers, and advertising executives of the bustling Chelsea publishing world.

According to sources at the venerable late night hangout for wannabe models, Ms. Cummings had just come from a freebie gig *as a volunteer at a Young Metropolitans League's charity bash, where she worked the crowd of trust-fund babies, selling $100 raffle tickets to benefit the Pets Without Partners Fund. The Upper East Side organization helps find homes for the stray animals of East Hampton, Long Island. Seems there's a plethora of rich runaway pets roaming the dunes.*

"OhMYGOD Dana was like all wound up," said Rhonda Schier, 21, a co-worker of Ms. Cummings. "Like she was telling everyone how she'd just come from this charity thing and like how Bradford Lawson himself told her she was like going to be the like Next Big Thing at Lawson Worldwide. You know, she was still wearing the outfit she modeled in. Ohmygod, I can't believe she was killed wearing it."

According to sources close to the investigation, Ms. Cummings was murdered shortly after leaving the Mocha Shoppe. Although the police are not commenting on the investigation, The Journal has been informed that Ms. Cummings was stabbed at the base of the neck with a sharp instrument, possibly an ice pick. The fatal wound pierced straight up from the back of the victim's neck into the brain.

As seen in The New York Journal EXCLUSIVE CRIME-SCENE PHOTO, whoever committed this heinous crime took their time to place the still warm corpse of Dana Cummings in a very high fashion pose.

I examined the photograph. Cummings' body lay face up, head arched back against a gray carpet, legs spread about ten inches apart. A black dress, pulled thigh-high, exposing a peek of the dark green band of her otherwise mint green stockings. Her long jet-black hair flared out away from her head. The right arm was bent. Her slender fingers almost touching the right ear. The left arm was fully extended, palm open. Above the left shoulder, blood soaked a heavy dark circle into the carpet.

Click.

APRIL 25, 2006
FASHION KILLER STRIKES AGAIN!

Ann Van Huy, 19, second victim of the macabre Fashion Killer, was found dead this morning at 3:23 AM in her West 21st Street apartment. Just a short walk from where Ms. Van Huy, the American-born daughter of Vietnamese immigrants, attended daily classes at The Fashion Institute of Technology.

Ms. Van Huy's brain, like that of the Fashion Killer's first victim, Dana Cummings, was pierced by an ice pick. Once again the victim was posed for a high fashion shoot...

I examined *The New York Journal* "Exclusive Crime Scene Photograph." This time the victim was on her side, lying on a stripped-down bed. She wore a tight, sleeveless black minidress, much like the kind I remembered the beautiful French-Vietnamese women wearing in the bars of Saigon. The only piece of bedding, other than the bare mattress Ann Van Huy lay on, was a puffy down pillow wedged between her bare, smooth legs. The pillow was silk-red. So was the thin line of blood running down Ms. Huy's shoulder.

I scrolled.

Embedded in the article was another photograph of Ann Van Huy. High school graduation. The face model-perfect. And something else—the fair complexion inherited from a hundred years of intermarriages with the French.

I scrolled.

"We give her good American name, Ann," the *Journal* quoted the victim's mother. "She our first born here in safe America."

Maybe it was in their DNA? Or just was in their legacy of living with fear? Whatever, I knew the Vietnamese to be a strong people. I knew Ann Van Huy's mother would learn to endure the loss of her daughter, as she had learned to endure many other losses. I also knew the mother would endure even better once I got my hands on the ice-picking bastard.

Click.

JUNE 23, 2006.
FASHION KILLER TAKES THIRD VICTIM!

Moleece Montrel, 19, was found dead at 2:26 AM in the West 14th loft she shared with Ms. Rachel Orloff, an independent filmmaker.

Ms. Montrel, a rising star at Lawson Worldwide, and newest client of Kirk and Devon Public Relations, was last seen modeling a Fargo-designed death dress in front of a Cadillac Escalade The Young Metropolitans League had up for auction at their Gamboling for Tots Without Fathers Gala held last night at the Grand Hyatt.

No one at Lawson Worldwide was available for comment. And repeated calls by The New York Journal to Virginia Kirk-Lawson's (Mrs. Michael Lawson) offices at Kirk and Devon have gone unanswered. Seems the Young Metropolitans are circling their stretch Hummers.

I scrolled further down, to the photograph of a young, anorexic-chic black woman, her face so thin and cheeks so drawn that, had I not already known I was looking at a corpse, I would have thought her dead anyway. She lay flat on her back on top of one of those 1950's style chrome-and-Formica wet bars, the black dress clinging to her plank-like torso. No stockings. Shoeless. Right arm dangling off the bar down between two chrome-and-leather stools like a squid ink-darkened strand of spaghetti.

Click.

SEPTEMBER 15, 2006
FASHION KILLER ON A RAMPAGE TAKES FOURTH VICTIM!!!
EXCLUSIVE CRIME SCENE PHOTOGRAPH!
MS. CANDICE NOLEN

CLICK...I closed the browser.

There had to be a message somewhere in these pictures, but whatever it was sure beat the hell out of me. The photographs didn't belong, as Dent had said, in *Harper's Bazaar* as much as they belonged in *Mortuary Bizarre.*

I leaned back from the screen, stretched my arms, and gazed through the library's arched windows. Outside, street lamps lighted the cobble sidewalk running along the Fifth Avenue side of Central Park. What time was it? Nine-twenty!

I stood up. Felt my knees crack. I was no closer to finding The Fashion Killer than when I had started. I pressed the mouse button and the computer screen went dark.

I left now for the last place Candice was seen alive.

SIX

THE LINE OF PEOPLE STRETCHED to the end of the block, then faded into the shadow at the turn of the corner.

Last week the rope wasn't red velvet, it was crime-scene yellow, and I was ushered through the main entrance of the Hotel Victory without protest. This time I crossed Tenth Avenue, knowing that if I wanted get past the front door of the Hotel's Club Faux Pas I'd need to place a Ben Franklin discreetly into the palm of the bald bouncer holding a clipboard.

I dug inside my pants pocket, feeling my money clip with the tip of my fingers, when I saw the bald bouncer—noticing now the diamond studs in each of his earlobes—staring down at an expensively clad short middle-aged man. The man was fondling the ass of a blond knockout that would never pass for his wife with one hand, and offering cash to baldy with the other. "If y'all offerin' me money, old man," Baldy said, loud enough for everyone in line to get his point, "then for sure you don't belong inside."

The short man, who was about to open his mouth and put on a show for his girlfriend, hesitated, came to his senses, and muttered in a face-saving voice, "Lets get out of here, I'll take you to a real class joint. Hog's Head."

Baldy was too busy saying "Next" to hear the little philanderer from Hackensack.

A boat-long white stretch Hummer pulled up to the curb. Heads peered out from the line, yet not a person dared move for fear of forfeiting a precious position. Two thin, ash-blond nymphets, all legs, slid from the vehicle. Cell phones waved and clicked photos, capturing the moment as the two sophomorically posed for the crowd. With sycophant timing, an entourage of young poured from the Hummer, nudging their brainless twin trophies towards the velvet rope. With a siren-pitched unison, the nymphets wailed an extended "Hiiiiii Ernie," and the bald bouncer smiled so wide his diamond studs got lost somewhere behind his cherubic cheeks as he lifted the rope. And there I stood, out of sync, stuck in another time, fingering a wad of cash in my pocket when I heard her voice.

"Jack? Whadaya doin' here?"

"Maria?"

"How ya feelin' Jack?"

"Been better," I answered with a reflex smile.

Maria Maglio could do that—force a smile from a guy even when he tried hard not to.

The circles I frequented thought of people like Maria—with her "youse guys" and "ain'ts," "ya knows" and "forgetaboutits" and her constant mixing of tenses—unsophisticated. But I knew that, if only those snobs could get past the vernacular, they could hear her wisdom.

"Soooo Jack? I mean, I can't believe you into clubbing and all."

"Just looking around. Wanted to see what Candice's world was like. You know what I mean."

Maria smiled at the way I said, "You know what I mean." She thought it cute when her stiff boss tried to act like a regular person.

"Can't get past the big guy, huh?" she said.

"I saw some Joe Blow tourist try to slip baldy some green."

"Forgetaboutit! Can't buy 'em. The bosses do them right, ya know what I mean," she smiled again. "Anyways, it's a power thing with them bouncers."

Maria grabbed my arm, pulling me along like a lost puppy.

The keeper of the gate lifted the velvet rope.

"Thanks Ernie," Maria smiled. And even Ernie couldn't help from cracking a smile from the corner of his mouth. And then he was quick to return his face back to the hard stare of a hit man, ready to snub out the "Next" in line.

There had to be six hundred people pressed together on the dance floor. Men with men, women with women, and even men with women, all humping to a DJ's beat unfamiliar to me.

Above the ear-shattering din Maria shouted, "Come on Jack," and tried pulling me onto the dance floor.

She was so young, so full of life. So happy. I'd be lying if I told you I'd never noticed her body before, or how sexy she was. Andy and I spoke our share of locker room remarks concerning Maria's lovely tits and great ass. And how her early morning workouts at the gym across from Smoothe Press should be made mandatory for all our female employees. No, we were not above such crude expressions of male bonding. But always inside me, I knew that other jerks were saying the same juvenile remarks about Candice.

Maybe it was some kind of male reflex action to the sight of something a man knows is strictly off-limits. But as crude as the remarks might rightly have sounded to anyone overhearing us, we still thought of Maria as Tony Maglio's little girl.

Tony was press foreman, and he had asked if his kid could work the summer in the pressroom with him. "We can always use a good Go-fa," he said.

Andy laughed. "Tony, you're the foreman, you need a Go-Fa, then go hire any Go-fa you want."

That was ten years ago. Two years later Tony died from cancer.

I smiled down at Maria, hearing Andy's laughter in my head, and said, "I don't dance."

Maria must have sensed the awkwardness her boss was feeling being with her in such a place. She slid her hand out of mine.

"Go ahead, enjoy yourself. I'll be okay," I said.

"Don't dare leave without me," she said, giving me a look that is natural in every woman. Candice could give me that same look when she was only six, and Uncle Jack would be putty in her hands.

"I won't," I promised.

Maria turned away and then, remembering something, she turned around, pulled a label from her purse, peeled off its adhesive back and pressed the label against my lapel. "It's a VIP pass," she said, rushing off to join the humpers.

How she'd gotten past the velvet rope, and how she came to possess VIP privileges, made me think there was much more to Maria than I had ever imagined. She didn't get into Club Faux Pas because of her body. Ernie had turned away other knockouts from the door. Maria got in because she had the right connections. I was very impressed with our little "Go-Fa."

I hit the bar for a Chivas, somehow managing to get my order past the five-deep crowd shouting to the staff of Mr. Body Beautiful bartenders serving up martinis in every color.

I took a slug of my own poison and headed to the VIP section, bumping and banging off a tight maze of tables and asses along the way.

This bouncer was dressed a bit more formally than Ernie. He had on a black tuxedo. Instead of a starched, stiff white shirt, he wore a black crew neck sweater, exposing neck muscles as thick as elevator cables. Perched at the top of three steps leading up to the coveted VIP section, he resembled a huge peregrine falcon overlooking the dance floor.

The Falcon glanced at my sticker. Paused. Cocked his head. This time the velvet rope I passed through was gold.

Club Faux Pas was sprinkled with enough middle-aged men so that I didn't feel totally out of place. But nobody seemed to notice me anyway as I moved through the room slowly, toting my drink, and smiling like an idiot.

It wasn't hard to spot the offspring of the super-rich holding court at the tables. Most of the women were either vegan bulimic or carried McDonald's midriffs. They seemed just a few years away from their first Botox injections. The men were all the same—weak.

One young man raised a Coors Light bottle over his unkempt hair calling out to the dance floor, where the two nymphets had sandwiched a tall, big-jawed, redheaded dyke wearing hip-high stiletto-heeled black leather boots. "Hey Trish," he called out. "How 'bout rubbing that pussy up against me."

The Falcon cocked a cold, hard stare that read like a warning of just how much he'd enjoy tossing Mr. Coors Light spoiled rich ass out onto Tenth Avenue.

It was then when I realized these wafer-board nymphets were the Internet-famous, semi-porn home video Baxter sisters, Trisha and Colette. Their father, Colin Baxter the Third, part of the self-proclaimed North Shore blueblood set, whose carpetbagger grandfather, Colin the First, I now imagined spinning in his marble mausoleum at the way his well-planned bloodline had retro-trashed.

For close to an hour I watched the chaotic goings-on about me. The ice in my Chivas had melted to an amber murk when, for the third time that evening, I felt the gentleness of Maria's hand tugging my arm. "Come on," she said. "I want you to meet a few people."

We made our way over to the table where Coors Light sat.

Inside, I grimaced at the thought of having to meet the jerk; outside, I put on a sales-rep smile.

The jerk's name was Justin. I offered my hand. He shook it with a limp, damp noodle of a hand. He acted as if he was doing me a favor. I didn't bother offering my hand again to anyone as Maria introduced me around the table.

It took me a few tries before I could acclimate my hearing to make out at least some of the conversation around the table. A pretty young woman, wearing a black baseball cap with a bright orange Princeton P, and fixated on adjusting her long blond ponytail hanging through its back strap, said she'd heard that the girl killed last week was Michael's legal assistant.

Another woman, Amy, I think she was called, said: "I met the poor thing right here in Club Faux Pas the night she was murdered. Of course Michael was there too. It was all for charity, you know."

My jaw clenched at her damn patronizing use of the word "poor."

Maria's eyes caught mine.

I managed to force up again my sales-rep smile and said, "Doesn't it frighten you, Amy?"

"Frighten me," Amy looked around the table, laughing. "Why should I be frightened of anything?"

"Frightened," I said, "that it could have been you who was murdered instead of that poor girl."

Amy put on a quizzical face, making me think the young woman may have been feeling the strange sensation of her brain actually engaging a real thought for the first time.

"OhMYGOD!" she chirped in a singsong voice that hit me like nails across a blackboard. "Ohmygod! You're like sooo right." Now turning to P-Cap she added, "You know Michael was the one who invited me."

"You know like it could be kismet," another brat said. "The girl worked for Michael. I once dated Michael. And we all like know Michael."

The girls all ohmygodding with the same blackboard inflection.

"Like, what do they call it? You know...Ah. That Kevin Bacon thing."

"Six temperatures of separation."

"That's six degrees of separation," Coors Light snotted in. Surprising the hell out of me the kid knew anything at all.

The girl Coors Light had corrected blew him off with a "Whatever."

Maria shook her head at the sheer stupidity of the entire group.

"Well, you know that girl..."

"Candice." P-Cap broke in.

"Yeah, yeah, Candice," Amy continued. "She was only there to model the Fargo dress."

"Oh, Virginia's new boy-toy."

"Don't call him that. He's nice," interjected another shrill voice. Angelica—or was her name Angie? I was having trouble distinguishing the shrills. Their voices were as interchangeable as singers in a Broadway Jukebox musical.

"Like," Amy said, "Michael told me that this Candice chick had once did some kind of modeling."

"I mean, like Michael didn't really want her there," P-Cap said. "He only pushed her into doing the party to get Virginia off his back."

"Yeah," Amy said. "What is that woman's problem?"

"Virginia?" P-Cap smirked.

"There's a fuckin' match made in heaven for ya," Amy quipped.

"Talk about gold digging," Angelica snapped. "Bitch goes from Production Assistant to the boss's son's wife to getting her own public relations firm. All in like what? —two fucking years."

"You gotta give it to her though, her pussy must know some pretty good tricks," one girl said.

Michael Lawson is one hot catch," said some McDonald chubette, looking just so ravishing in pelvis-hugging pants and a gold ring piercing her tire-tube tummy.

P-Cap, clearly agitated with her ponytail, stood up. "Oh I've had enough of this shit-talk," she quipped. "I'm out of here."

She ran off down the steps, passing the gold velvet rope, finally giving up with the ponytail and removing her P-cap in total frustration.

Ms. Big Mac flipped her middle finger at P-Cap's back, commenting to the others, "Bitch must be on the rag."

Angelica squinted, as if recalling an image to her mind. "You know something, I think that Asian chick was also a guest of Michael's at the Texas Hold-em for...for...whatever-the-fuck-it-was benefit. And like wasn't she prancing *her* fuckin' ass around in a Fargo, too?"

"That's right." Coors Light brightened up, speaking for the first time since his six-degrees high point. "She most fuckin' definitely was." He pointed his beer bottle again towards the dance floor. "I bet Asian twat rubbing is better than Baxter twat rubbing."

I had had enough of the brainless trust-fund brats. I gave Maria the high sign.

She picked up on it.

"Come on boss," she said, glancing at the choir around the table. "Let me get you home before you scare the girls to death."

"Ooo, Maria's going to *tuck* her boss in," Mr. Coors Light said.

I was a split-second away from doing something stupid when Maria side-stepped in front of me, leaned over and grabbed Coors Light's crotch.

The jerk flinched. Rose half-up from his chair.

Maria pressed her left hand down on his shoulder. Pushed her face right up to the blue-eyed blond A-hole's face, tightened the vise-grip she had on his balls, and in a low, threatening whisper, said, "You ain't gonna be usin' this little twat-rubber tonight."

We walked away, leaving Mr. Coors Light, bent at the knees and looking like a busted flamingo lawn ornament.

Giving Maria one hell of a grin, the Falcon held up the gold rope for us.

SEVEN

Out on Tenth Avenue I laughed for the first time in more than a week.

"Maria, you're some piece of work."

"Oh, those guys are just a bunch of A-holes."

"So what the hell are you doing hanging with them?" I asked, looking over Maria's shoulder for a cab.

"Kicks."

"Not for nothing, Maria, but how'd you come to hang with them in the first place?"

"Not for nothing!" Maria cocked her head. "What you really mean is how'd Tony's kid come to be with those rich-bitches?"

"Don't bust my balls. You're not exactly a Princeton preppie."

Now Maria was laughing. "Whadaya kiddin'. You just ain't seen me in my Princeton cap, that's all."

"That cap went real well with the long slit in that airhead's dress."

"Come on Jack. Whatcha really doin' here, checking out the scene of the crime or somethin'?"

"Or somethin'."

"Jack, don't bullshit a bullshitter. You're goin' after the Fashion Killer. Ain'tcha?"

I made my best Freddy-the-doorman move. "Cab!"

A yellow cab pulled up to the curb. "Get in," I said, holding open the door.

"Where to?" the cabbie grunted.

"Your place," I said to Maria.

She arched her eyebrow. "Oh, yeah."

"Quit kidding."

"West Broadway and Spring," Maria told the cabbie.

The cab pulled away from Club Faux Pas.

"So what are you doing out alone anyway? Couldn't find a date?"

"Have had it up to here with too many jerks," Maria said, holding her hand up to her chin.

Maria sure did have knack for finding jerks. She married one. A good-looking kid named Joey Ramone. Didn't last long. The guy got on the wrong side of Andy Smoothe. Which is a bad place for anyone to be.

Ramone started out as a messenger at Smooth Press and, when he married Maria, Andy promoted the kid to the prep room. So what happens? Joey Ramone begins thinking he's a big man. Has more money then a bum like him should ever have, and starts in with the 3 B's: boozing, bookies and bimbos.

At home, Maria reads Joey the riot act. Tempers flare. Maria doesn't come in to work for a week. Joey says she's down with the flu. When she finally does show up back at work, Andy spots she's wearing dark sunglass and a little too much makeup.

Andy gets Maria out for coffee before anyone else catches a glimpse of the Max-Factored bruises.

Over bagels and coffee the kid breaks down in tears and gives up what's been going on at home. Andy hands Maria a couple hundred and says go shopping. Then he heads back for the prep room.

The way I got the story, Andy escorted the bum down the back stairwell. Twenty minutes later, Andy returns and tells the receptionist Joey's gone for the day.

And as far I know, the story ended right there. Except that Andy's lawyer got Maria an annulment in a New York minute.

And as for Joey Ramone, I figured the bum just left work that day through the back door and decided to pack it up for Siberia. Or anyplace else far from the reach of Andy Smoothe.

The cab turned onto West Broadway. "Do you know this Fargo guy?" I asked.

"About a month ago I saw Virginia dragging Fargo around like a teddy bear at Bungalow 8."

Bungalow 8! I was discovering a Maria I didn't know existed, wondering again how she was able to get past the velvet ropes of the most exclusive celeb-clubs in the city.

"What's Virginia Lawson, his keeper?"

"Virginia *Kirk*-Lawson is the mouth half of Kirk and Devon Public Relations," Maria said. "Loretta Devon is the brains half. Maria smiled. "And Fargo, AKA one Vinny Fargomatto from Brooklyn, is going to be their first big thing."

"What's this Fargo like?"

"Guy's a real player. And he likes swinging both ways, Y'know what I mean?"

"A lot of that going around these days."

Maria smirked at her boss. "Anyways, Fargo's goin' through a nasty breakup with his two ex-business partners."

I cocked my head.

"A husband and wife team. I don't remember their names or nothin'. Except, I remember the wife cursing out Fargo in some kind of thick foreign accent the night he punched her out at Faux Pas—"

"Wait a minute! You telling me Fargo's into beating up women?"

Maria shrugged and said, "Fargo's told everyone he was going after the husband and the bitch just got in the way. Whatever, the fight made it onto Page Six and all."

"Lawsuits?"

"How do I know? What am I a lawyer or somethin'? Anyways, the three partners used to shack up together in an apartment they also used as their design studio down on the Lower Eastside somewheres. I heard three of 'em slept together on a big waterbed in the middle of the place.

"Anyways, since Fargo went and dumped them and signed with Kirk and Devon—and if you ask me, I think the whole idea to dump 'em was put into his head by that Virginia bitch—Fargo's the one getting all the attention. And Virginia's been using the Young Metropolitans Galas like a runway for her client's designs. Except Fargo's exes are going 'round saying he's been stealing all the designs from before the breakup."

"Think maybe the husband and wife team got a wild hair up their asses?" I asked.

"And they start whacking innocent models? What's the purpose of that?"

"Maybe to send a message."

The cab pulled up in front of Maria's place.

"Message?" Maria pushed open the cab's rear door. "What kind of message?"

"Don't get caught dead wearing a Fargo," I said.

EIGHT

WHEN SHE TOUCHED MY HAND at the funeral, whispering, "Call me if I can do anything," I had bent forward thanking the little white-haired lady, giving her a gentle kiss on her cheek. On the Saturday morning after my night out with the brats and Maria, I called B.P.

"Sure, kid, come on out to the country tomorrow for brunch," she had said without any hesitation.

It had been a long while since I had hit the open road. When the expressway traffic thinned out just past Riverhead, I pushed the speedometer needle to 115. The rushing wind slipped over the surface of my Jaguar XJ8 as silently as silk across glass.

On another morning I would have dug getting caught up in the Zen of the wind, the road, the endless blue Long Island sky; the miles of vineyards touched by the tease of salt air drifting in off the Atlantic Ocean. But not this morning. This morning, my mind was racing as fast as the Jag's pistons. I knew I had to get into the trust-fund brat world of The Young Metropolitans. And no one could get me into that world faster then B.P.

B.P.'S PERSONAL ASSISTANT, Bertha, a short, stout, no-nonsense woman, led me into the den.

The matriarch of Manhattan Event Planners sat behind a white, gold trimmed, antique desk, holding a Bloody Mary, and peering through red-rimmed bifocals at the Sunday *New York Times* Style Section.

"Look at this bullshit, will you!" She turned the paper around for me to see, her blue eyes radiating over the bifocals. "As long as they can get a hot designer's outfit to shake their ass in they'll front for any cause."

I leaned over the *Times* and kissed my friend's cheek. The hint of her Giorgio perfume smelled nice.

I owed B.P. much. Andy did too. We were her exclusive printers.

"How you holding up, kid?" She always called me kid.

Somehow the clock had ticked away. I felt my face scraping against the brick wall of mid-life. I was standing before my mentor now at exactly the same age she had been when we had first met twenty-seven years before.

And here, my mentor, who was always addressed only by her initials, sat behind her desk with the un-Botoxed confidence of a self-made woman. Thin branches spread from the corners of B.P.'s eyes. Shallow furrows etched across her forehead. Women with class age well: Bacall, Hepburn.

"Pour yourself a Bloody Mary, sit down and tell me what you need."

The Bloody Mary was fresh, the chair firm. B.P. wasn't someone to cover in bullshit. I got straight to the point.

"I'm going to kill whoever murdered Candice."

Looking down into her drink as if reading tea leaves she asked: "Jackie, are you willing to do the time?"

"For what? Ridding the city of a terrorist?"

"Don't be naive. Depending on the direction the political wind is blowing, you can just as easily go down as a goat, as come up a savior. I know the Mayor, he doesn't like being showed up."

"I don't give a damn about the Mayor. Right now I need a fix on these trust-fund babies. Whatever the reason, this killer is traveling in their world and I need to become a part of it fast."

B.P. remained silent.

I released a long sigh.

"Look," I said. "All four victims modeled dresses by some designer called Fargo at a Young Metropolitans League event on the night they were murdered. Someone hates Fargo, or hates these brats, enough to commit murder."

"Maybe both," B.P. said.

"And Michael Lawson, in one way or another, has had a connection to the victims."

"Maybe it's Michael someone hates," B.P. offered.

"Or maybe he's the one who's full of hate."

B.P. twisted her lips. "I think you're way off base with that one."

"What do you know about the Lawson kid?"

"Jackie, these kids are suckled from birth on platinum tits. Their entire world is a VIP room. They slither through Dalton, or Horace Mann, or Lenox, or some other exclusive private school, then their parents buy their way into Daddy's or Mommy's alma mater, where the girls complete their bitchification, and the boys hone their drinking and networking skills. But the Lawson kids are interesting."

I had all but forgotten Bradford Lawson had two sons.

"You know the younger son, Paul, pissed Daddy off when he enlisted."

"You couldn't tell that by the way Bradford boasted in the papers of how his son was a great American to have volunteered to serve in Iraq."

"That's the front Bradford puts up. What he really did was cut the kid off. Right now all Paul has is his military paycheck."

"That just might make a man out of at least one Lawson."

"Michael may have a shot at becoming a man too, if he ever gets out from under his father's thumb. He actually got accepted to Princeton on his brains, not Daddy's pull. And graduated Yale Law near the top of his class."

"What about his wife's thumb?"

"There's a winner for you," B.P put down her Bloody Mary. "Virginia Kirk's *pleasant* attitude got her tossed first from Lenox, and then from Horace Mann.

"When no other prep school would accept her foul-mouth antics, the family got private tutors. Then sent her to Penta, an exclusive university in the South of France known to encourage the recruitment—at a hefty tuition—of young, rich incorrigibles. There Virginia took up with some Euro-trash. Spent most her time snorting coke, and jaunting between Milan, London and Paris."

"You never surprise me with what you know about everyone."

"It's my business to know, Jackie," B.P. said, with a tough grin. "Still, Virginia got a degree of some kind. Stayed abroad for a few more months until finally the Euro-trash boys she'd been screwing got tired of her attitude and snubbed her out like a spent American cigarette. When she returned home she somehow, I really don't know how, but she got a meaningless job at Lawson Worldwide."

"And Bradford Lawson wasn't upset that Virginia married Michael?"

"Bradford likes the fact that Kirk money is old-line, made when Virginia's great-great-grandfather bought up hundreds of acres of Brooklyn farmland in the anticipation of a Bridge being eventually built. Whatever, it happened, and the kids had a winter wedding down in Palm Beach."

"Margo Largo?"

"Where else?" B.P. smirked. "When they got back from their honeymoon in St. Tropez, Virginia couldn't stay on as a meaningless employee working for her husband, so she did what a lot of her contemporaries who love to yak away idle hours on their cell phones do—she became a publicist.

"God, Jackie. There are about seven or eight of these bitches, all referring to each other as"—B.P. held her hands up in mocking air-quotes—"Like sisters." And Jackie, the truth be known, these little bitches really can make or break any rising star in this town. Shit. If it wasn't for this sisterhood of bitches feeding *The New York Post*, Page Six would be blank."

Pausing to sip her Bloody Mary, I noticed now scorn in her eyes as she held the glass.

"And Virginia Kirk Lawson is the biggest bitch of all." B.P. set the glass down carefully, and continued filling me in.

"Two years ago Virginia found a young pixie of a girl in Penn Station waiting for an Amtrak back to some no-name town in

Maryland and swept the kid up with dreams of stardom. She started promoting her around town as the next supermodel.

"She got the girl designer clothes. Placed her on the arm of every hot young second-rate actor in town. Even let this kid from the sticks stay at the Kirk's East Hampton estate.

"And then when this train-station nymphet got caught drunk and sucking on the dick of one of the "sisterhood's" husbands, Virginia bounced her next big thing's ass back to no-namesville by calling the kid a 'no-talent cunt' to every gossip columnist from New York to St. Tropez."

"Seems Virginia had her hopes on making Candice her next big thing," I said. "But, my niece wanted nothing to do with it."

B.P. arched an eyebrow.

"Don't look at me that way," I said. "I got the drift from the brat pack that Candice was just appeasing her boss so that his pestering wife would get off his back about pushing his secretary into a modeling career. Besides, Candice had tried modeling once before and hated it."

My mentor flipped open a white leather-bound Filofax, wetting the tip of her index finger to turn the pages.

"If you want to penetrate this group," she said, "you're going to have to get on the guest list for one of their pet causes."

While B.P. searched for my perfect coming-out event, I cocked my head looking down at the Styles section lying on the desk.

The weekly montage of superficial smiles of the rich and powerful attending benefit galas, were all numbered and keyed to captions that read like a Park Avenue society directory. A few faces were recognizable old-money patriarchs and matrons. A Rockefeller at the Modern. A Whitney at the Met. Even an Astor.

And then there were the bright young faces of the new money. I wondered who would be the next Brook Astor, or the next Jock Whitney, out of this crowd of Young Metropolitans.

"These parties are nothing more than media events to keep the rich in the public eye," I scowled, folding over the *Times*. "Do any of them really give a damn about the charity they let add their names to the stationery masthead?"

B.P. placed down her diary, removed her bifocals. She looked at me straight on.

"Listen Jackie, let me warn you now. If there is a connection between these murders and the brats, the rich will keep it within their little platinum cocoon. They're not going to have the murders of some working-class girls destroy their social standing."

B.P. returned the bifocals to the bridge of her nose, fingering the pages of her Filofax again.

"There's an event November 6th," she said, pointing to an entry. "I'll get you an invitation. You'll buy a whole table worth of tickets. It'll get your ass kissed enough so that you can get closer to those you need to.

"And Jackie," she added, pointing her finger at me. "You had better fill the table with young people."

"And how do you suppose I accomplish this?"

Her blue eyes peered up over the red rims of the bifocals at me, her stuffy, middle-aged surrogate son, and sighed. "I'll make some calls."

Her assistant stepped into the room. "Excuse me."

"Yes, Bertha."

"Jenna has just arrived."

"I'll be right there."

"How's your granddaughter doing?"

"Great. Really. The light of my life."

"What? Eighteen, nineteen now?"

"Twenty-three!"

I stood up.

"Well, I'd better go. Thanks for everything, B.P."

"One more thing, Kid."

"What's that?"

"Have you got yourself a young chippy hidden away somewhere?"

B.P. didn't wait for my reply. "Find one!" she said.

NINE

MONDAY I SHOWED UP AT Smoothe Press at my usual time of 8 AM. Andy arrived at his usual time: Ten.

I stared at Andy sitting there behind a scarred oak desk from the 1940s. The same desk where his old man dropped dead, leaving his son a business he didn't know how to run. That's when I stepped in the picture. I was an accountant then and Smoothe Press was my first, and as it turned out, my last client.

I moved near the massive antique manual printing press Andy kept in his spacious office. I figured it was a good idea not to be too close to my partner when I hit him with my crazy plan.

I began slowly by telling Andy about my meeting with Dent and how the murders were somehow connected to the trust-fund babies. I told him about my casing out Club Faux Pas. He grinned at how easily Maria had gotten me past the velvet rope saying, "Kid must know the right people."

When I was finished Andy took his turn. "You think I wouldn't like to get this fuck too?" he said. "Shit, I'd stick him in the electric chair and flip the switch myself. But hell, Jack, we're not cops. And we're not vigilantes. We're just a couple of regular working stiffs. So why don't you let this Detective Dent do his job?"

"I got the feeling the guy wants me in."

"Why? He say something to you?"

"No."

"Jesus, Jack! You dress in expensive English custom-made suits. Drive a $100,000 sports car. So what do you think—now you're some kind of James fuckin' Bond or something? Forget about it. You're Jack Centaur. Middle-aged, out of shape, number crunching, goddamn Chief Financial Officer."

I walked away from the antique press. Stood square-footed, facing my partner. "I didn't come in here for your permission. I came in to tell you what you need to know."

Andy cocked his head. "Sit the hell down."

I didn't budge.

"Look, B.P. is arranging for me to buy a table at a Young Metropolitans benefit next month."

"What are you going to do, fill it with all your old fart cronies from that historic club of yours? It'll look like the chaperone's table at a school dance."

"She's taking care of that too."

"Oh, I see, she's going to wallpaper your table with the young and beautiful?" Andy smirked. "And you'll be the one, lone old fart."

"Maria knows these brats from the club scene."

"So what's that got to do with the price of tea in China?"

"I'm going to ask Maria to front as my girlfriend."

"What!"

Here it comes, I thought, watching my partner fly up from the chair.

"You've got to be out of your fuckin' mind! If Tony were still alive he'd have your head for this."

"She'll be in no danger."

Andy rolled his eyes. "Famous last words."

I'm six-foot-one, yet Andy towered over me. "You want to sit back down now," I said. "I'm getting a pain in my neck looking up at you."

"So you're going to play Big Daddy with Maria." Andy grimaced, pulling his chair back into place and sitting again behind the old desk. "And this is not going to look phony?"

It was now safe for me to sit down too, so I slid into one of the two old swivel chairs in front of the desk. "There were so many Big Daddies at Faux Pas Friday night it looked like a father-daughter dance."

"I still don't get it," Andy said, leaning back in his father's worn leather chair. "You think the Fashion Killer is going to be at this party?"

"Maybe."

"Yeah, and maybe wearing a sign too. Just to make it easier for you."

"All right already. Get off my fucking case. I need to start somewhere. Maybe I'll hear something from one of these kids that will help me. I don't know. But I've got to do something. I've just got to. I can't sit still."

Andy frowned, knowing he could not stop me.

"Maria's agreed to this plan of yours?"

Now it was me rolling the eyes.

"You haven't broken this shit to her yet. Oh, this will be fun. I can see it now. ' Come into my office, Maria, I want to shack up with you. "

"Stop being such an asshole. You know I wouldn't lay a glove on the kid."

"What are you going to do when you're around those brats, hold her hand? Big Daddies like feeling up their little girls."

"I guess I'm just going to show them what class is. Teach 'em how to act in public. They sure could use a lesson."

"Class! Class! You really are fuckin' crazy."

"Maybe I'll give her a hug. If she'll let me."

"Won't look kosher. You're going to have to act like a middle-aged fool. Be all over her if you want them to drop their guard around you. And I don't like the thought of you being all over her. I'll tell you that right now!"

"Middle-aged fool. There's something you should know a bit about."

Andy smirked, "Et tu, Brutus."

"Hell, you were the one who was screwing around on his wife with a twenty-two-year-old."

"Deidre was some twenty-two-year-old," Andy smiled wide.

"So I guess I've learned from the best how to play the fool," I said, getting up.

Andy let out a deep sigh that lifted up the edge of one of the pink telephone message slips piled on his desk. "I'm warning you. You're making a huge mistake."

IF THERE WERE ever an Olympic event for switchboarding, Maria would win it hands down. Headset pressed against her ears, she punched the line lights with her long fingers as fast as the lights blinked. "Good Mornin', Smoothe Press. Who's callin', I'll put ya through." Sometimes she'd break her rhythmic candor with an abrupt "NOT interested."

Sensing she was being watched, Maria looked up. She smiled a little bit wider for her boss as she answered yet another call with the swiftness of a thoroughbred running at Belmont.

I cocked my head toward the conference room.

Maria's green eyes twinkled with an acknowledging wink that contained more class than any five of those trust-fund babies would ever possess in ten lifetimes.

I sat in one of the twelve worn leather chairs that surrounded the oak conference table and waited.

Olga entered the conference room carrying the lid from a corrugated box of copying paper filled with triangle-cut sandwiches sealed in plastic wrap, bags of potato chips, several cans of diet Coke, and a couple of bottles of spring water. She hesitated, surprised by the sight of me sitting there, alone.

I rose to help her with the box, but she had it down on the table before I was half-standing. Olga smiled again, turned and left. It was 11:20 AM. I had forty minutes to make my plea before the staff gathered for lunch.

Maria wore a sleeveless pale blue cotton jersey shift that clung to the curves of her body like a T-shirt ready to be wetted. The kid swiveled out one of the leather chairs from beneath the conference table and manipulated her body like a gymnast mounting a stationary horse. Her long, feminine fingers grasped the armrests. The strength of her flexing biceps proved the benefits of all those morning workouts as she hung suspended there in mid-air. Watching the ease at which she curled up her equally muscular bare legs, slowly lowering herself onto the leather cushion, I felt the distance between our ages.

"What's up?" she asked.

I held my words for a moment, considering Andy's warning. Then I said, "I need you to do me a favor."

"Sure. Whatcha need?"

"It's going to be embarrassing for you. It's going to be embarrassing for me."

Maria looked puzzled.

"I want you to pretend to be my girlfriend."

"In front of those jerks you met at the club?"

"I need a date. I bought a table at the Young Metropolitans League's next benefit."

The two emerald pools that had twinkled at me from the phone bank only moments ago had turned serious.

"If you think it's gonna help you find the scumbag who killed Candice," she said, her voice strained with an anger. "Whadaya want me to be, some kind of target for The Fashion Killer?"

"No! Nothing like that. I don't want to put you in any jeopardy. I just want to keep it simple. Let everyone think I'm just a dumb old fart being soaked for his bread by—"

"By a poor bimbo from Brooklyn."

I leaned back in my chair, feeling ashamed of seeming so shallow to her.

Maria reached over and touched my hand. "I know you would never think that way about me," she said. "And I surely don't think of myself in that way. But, that is what *they* think of me."

I pressed my lips.

"It's okay, Jack. I'll do it if you really feel it will help us catch the Fashion Killer."

Somewhere out of my notice, deep within the catacomb of Smoothe Press, Tony Maglio's little girl had morphed into a woman.

TEN

THE BOLD BRASS LETTERS ON the glass doors read: LAWSON WORLDWIDE MEDIA

Below, in smaller type: A LIMITED LIABILITY CORPORATION

We'll see how limited, I thought, and pushed open the doors.

The reception area walls were hung with museum-quality paintings. The kind of stuff I knew was bought at uptown galleries and increased in value every year, while being depreciated on the company's books like worn office furniture.

I walked up to the blond knockout sitting behind the mahogany reception desk and said, "I'm here to see Michael Lawson."

"And you are?" Her smile as phony as her bonded white teeth.

"Mr. Centaur."

With a few quick keystrokes she referred blankly to her computer screen, saying, "Mr. Centaur? I don't see that you have an appointment today with Michael."

"Then make one."

She looked up again. She wasn't smiling anymore.

I fingered the nameplate sitting on the desk. "And Ms. Lipshitz," I said. "I suggest you make it for right now."

The wannabe actress was about to call for security.

I dulled the edge off my voice. "Just tell Michael I'm Candice Nolen's uncle."

"Err," she flustered. "Michael hasn't arrived yet."

I was about to call Ms. Lipshitz' bluff when Michael Lawson strutted through the glass doors with all the brashness of inherited success, his jutting chin slicing the sterile office air like a surgeon's blade, his steel-gray eyes focused on the Blackberry he held out like Alice's looking glass.

I stepped away from the reception desk directly into the kid's path.

"Mr. Lawson," I said, my right hand offered. "Jack Centaur."

Michael Lawson stopped in half-stride, pulled his eyes from the Blackberry to see who the hell had the nerve to get into his face, then gave a quick questioning glance over to Ms. Lipshitz.

"Candice Nolen's uncle," Ms. Lipshitz whispered.

The kid was fast on his feet. He switched the Blackberry to his left hand and clasped my right with a lot more authority in it than the Coors Light kid at Club Faux Pas.

"Oh sure, Mr. Centaur," he smiled. "Candice said so many nice things about you."

I doubted whether my niece had ever mentioned having an uncle to her boss.

"She said a lot of nice things about you too," I bullshitted back, deciding to take the humble approach. "I need just a few minutes of your time…if you don't mind?"

"Well I do have a busy morning." He held up his Blackberry. "Yeah, all right." He turned to the wannabe. "Peggy, please push my two-o'clock to two-fifteen."

He turned, smiling magnanimously to me.

I replied with humility as phony as Lawson's two-o'clock, "That's so kind of you."

"Come, Mr. Centaur," Michael Lawson said, placing his hand, the Blackberry still in it, across my back, leading me through another set of glass doors.

My skin crawled under my suit. I'd play it this way for as long as I could. But I knew it was going to be hard to hold it up for an entire fifteen minutes.

On the other side of the glass doors we entered a large bullpen. Lawson escorted me through a maze of modular cubicles. To our left was a floor-to-ceiling wall of tinted glass. The view was of New Jersey.

My throat tightened when an image of Candice peering out from one of the cubicles to catch a glimpse of the action along the Hudson River jumped into my mind. She was wearing a phone headset, just another young woman with a full life ahead of her.

Michael Lawson held yet another glass door open, now we were entering his huge, sparsely furnished office. It too had a ceiling-to-floor wall of windows. The view was strictly uptown.

The kid waved for me to have a seat on a couch, as he walked behind the slab of white Italian marble he used for a desk. Michael Lawson sat himself down in one of those Herman Miller web-back chairs that cost a few grand and were supposed to allow a person to labor for hours without back fatigue. I couldn't picture this kid for the kind of person who needed such a chair. The desk didn't have any drawers. And the glass wastebasket beneath it was empty. The only item on the cold slab of a desk was a copy of the oversized, and overindulgent, magazine called Gotham.

Michael's crossed legs seemed to fit perfectly in with the Queen Anne curved legs of his desk. A metro-sexual, Candice had called her boss. Whatever the hell she had meant by that I wasn't really ever sure of until right then.

I looked over at the white leather couch Michael had offered to me, and sat myself down instead in one of two uncomfortable chrome-and-leather chairs in front of his desk.

Michael Lawson shrugged.

"I—"

"Just one sec," Michael cut me off, cradling the damn Blackberry now with both hands.

The kid could thumb-type faster then a touch typist using all ten fingers. While he hit the tiny keys he vocally annotated his written responses like a barroom quarterback calling audibles. "Fuck that," he grunted. "Up yours," he murmured. "You gotta be kidding me. No shot, a-hole."

Finally laying the Blackberry down on the slab of a desk, he looked over to me. "Shit, I get like a hundred fuckin' emails a day."

"I wouldn't know," I quipped. "I don't do email."

The kid's face went blank.

Our conversation began like a low-budget movie.

"I told the police everything I know," Lawson said.

"Now tell me," I countered.

"Well, it's like this," Michael leaned back in his expensive chair. "You do know that Ginny"—I shrugged my ignorance—"My wife Virginia Kirk Lawson"—Michael clarified—"She's one half of the P.R. firm Kirk and Devon?"

"So I've heard."

Michael continued. "Well, Ginny has like this unfuckin' believable knack for spotting opportunity. And she saw a great opportunity in your niece. I mean, like your niece could have made real megabucks with Ginny promoting her. Like Ginny has a line to every big editor and agent in town. The guys at Page Six like fall all over Ginny and her friends to get good shit to put in that column."

"So Ginny was all over Candice to sign up with Kirk and Devon?"

"And your niece wanted none of it." Lawson shook his head, incredulously. "But let me tell you something, my wife is a one real pain in the fuckin' A."

Michael picked up the Blackberry again and began thumbing it rapidly like a man addicted.

"Look," he continued, not looking up at me. "All Ginny wanted was for your niece to do one shoot. Do the shoot and get it over with, I told Candice. But she kept refusing."

"So you should have left it at that, and told your wife to fuck off."

Lawson smirked. "Yeah right. Anyway, what the hell did your niece have against money? I mean like if she took Ginny up, your niece would be partying in East Hampton and tripping down to Saint Tropez, instead of living with her mother in some apartment in Brooklyn."

My words crossed over the sandpaper of my drying throat as I spoke. "Maybe she didn't like what money and fame do to people."

"Like what?" Lawson replied, scrolling the damn Blackberry, not bothering to look up.

"With enough money you'll never have to put up with anyone's bullshit. And fame. Hell, like fame gets you past the velvet ropes."

Lawson lifted one hand from the Blackberry and pointed his finger pistol-like. Just the way his father did at photo ops. "Anyway, with Ginny representing her, and Lawson Worldwide Media setting up the gigs, your niece had a shot at being like the next big thing."

"But she didn't want it and you people just couldn't accept it. I mean, after all, you people always get what you want."

"Actually, I was like totally bored of it all. Just wanted Ginny off my fuckin' back. I said, look, Candice, just do this one time. Play model for one night. Wear the damn Fargo dress to the benefit. After that, I told your niece, if you still think you don't want the fame and glamour, like no one will bother you ever again."

"So you thought my niece could be seduced by the glamor of it all."

"Ginny said the girl wouldn't know what hit her. At the benefit she'd be hanging out with the hottest people in town. Candice would get a little stardust sprinkled on her, and she'd be hooked. Ginny said how couldn't she want to live that kind of life? The life of a *star*."

"But the plan didn't work. Did it?"

"No. Like the party was still going strong and Candice comes up to me and says she wants to go home."

"So then what happened?"

"I gave her the key-card to my suite so she could change her clothes."

"She wasn't leaving in the Fargo?"

"Nah, she said she hated wearing it."

"What did you do then?"

"When?"

"After you gave her your key."

"Me?"

I cocked my head.

"Like what? You think I killed her. Like I'm the fuckin' Fashion Killer?"

"So what did you do after you gave my niece your key?" I asked again.

"I…I…don't remember."

"Think."

"Um… Like I…uh stayed down in the club and partied." Lawson was thumbing the Blackberry feverishly. "Look, time's up. Like it's 2:25 already."

"Hey, A-hole." I clenched my fist. "Every victim seems to have been connected to your little fundraising club. You ever stop beating your Blackberry long enough to realize that, you putz?"

"Don't get pissed at me! I'm not responsible for your niece's death."

I sat in that stiff chair looking up at this silver spoon-fed chip off the old block behind that prissy desk with his I'm-above-it-all attitude.

Then the kid made a mistake. He stood up. He walked around to the front of the desk to show me the door. "I've got a meeting," he said.

I rose up from the stiff chair.

Once again Michael Lawson graciously offered his hand to me.

He started to say, "I'm sorry for your…" when I hit him with a right jab to the solar plexus. The punk doubled over. I yanked the twit's head up by its moussed blond hair, bringing my face to within a nostril hair of Lawson's and said through clenched teeth, "Stick this into your fucking Blackberry. You're covering up something and I'm going to find out what it is. And if it has anything to do with my niece's death I'm coming back here. And all your father's money won't be able to save you."

I let go of the kid's head, slipped a handkerchief from my inside breast pocket and wiped the mousse off my hand.

The kid managed to brace himself up against the marble desk with one hand. He was holding his gut with the other hand, struggling to catch a breath. The Blackberry lay on the floor. I crushed it with the hard leather heel of my double-E oxford and showed myself out of Lawson Worldwide Media.

ELEVEN

THE OFFICE OF KIRK AND Devon sat just six short blocks from Lawson Worldwide. I decided to make this my second unexpected cold call of the afternoon, see if maybe I could catch "Ginny" before her husband got to her. Although I was fairly certain the Lawson kid wasn't going to call his wife about our meeting. I had the distinct feeling Michael didn't like to talk to his wife unless he really had to.

The fist I had put into the kid's gut was the first time I had struck anyone since Vietnam. And I did not feel good about it. Didn't like it at all. Yet it needed to be done. The kid had to know Jack Centaur wasn't an ass-wipe he could dismiss like the emails on that damn Blackberry. Michael Lawson had to understand I wasn't going away. That I was after whatever he was hiding about the night Candice was murdered.

The building once housed a factory. The front door was gray steel, and locked. I pushed the intercom button for Kirk and Devon. To my surprise Loretta Devon buzzed me in as soon as she heard my name.

Inside the building I stood in an anteroom, a small elevator facing me. I stepped into the elevator, its metal walls speckled blue and white, like the inside of an old oven. The bank of buttons showed the building had just six floors. The button above number five read Penthouse. Above that was a key slot for access to the roof. I pressed five. The oven creaked up. The only break I got from my claustrophobia was watching the gray painted walls of each floor as they slowly passed my view through the elevator door's porthole window.

When I stepped onto the fifth floor I saw Loretta Devon standing in the doorway of her loft-slash-office. She had the soft, cocoa-butter skin of a Middle Eastern woman. Her cut-off black sweatshirt revealed a firm midriff. The cut-down sleeves, unraveled at the edges, showed her slight yet muscular arms. Her jeans slung so low only the joints of her pelvic bones kept her from being arrested for indecent exposure. A Bluetooth was stuck in her right ear, a cell phone clipped to her waistband. "I've put a kettle on," she said, waving me in. Her British accent was a welcomed respite from the high-pitched, snot voices of the Upper Eastside.

"Thank you. I'd love a cuppa," I said, Britishly.

Devon walked across the room ahead of me, her flip-flops patting gentle against the hardwood floor. Her firm legs filled the jeans in a way that forced a man to follow them right up to the curve of her ass. In mid-stride she stopped, turning to face me. A sudden twinkle came into her green eyes. Had she sensed me staring? I tried to force the flush of red from my cheeks. "Forgive me for my thoughtlessness," she said. "May I offer my condolences to you and your sister."

For the first time that day the conciliatory words didn't sound perfunctory.

"You're very kind. Thank you."

"I read in the *Journal* that the two of you are Candice's only family."

"Her father died when she was five."

"Yes, I read that too. So sorry." The kettle whistled. "Please have a seat."

I looked over to the glass dining room table covered with stacks of paper. I took a seat in a rattan chair, near what I figured had to be the social end of the workspace.

I had known the building before its conversion to loft apartments. It had housed a competitor of Smoothe Press who became a victim of the 1991 recession. Piping for the fire department's mandatory sprinkling system was still exposed along the high ceilings. The room once accommodated huge printing presses. Now the entire floor was open space, except for a fabric partition wall that ran three quarters the width of the loft. Behind the partition, I assumed, was Loretta Devon's bedroom.

"You are aware I work out with your girlfriend most mornings?" Devon asked over her shoulder, as she poured the boiling water from the kettle into a delicate china teapot. The back of her hair was neatly cut, and hung nice on the nape of her brown neck. The hair glistened black in the natural light of the sun-drenched room. The sweet hint of jasmine tea scented the air.

"Maria says you introduced her to the crowd at Club Faux Pas," I said.

"Yes. Brilliant coincidence. Don't you think?"

"What's that?"

"Maria and I should meet at the gymnasium and that your niece worked for my partner's husband."

"New York's a big city of small worlds," I said.

"Yes, you're quite right."

Loretta brought the pot of fresh brewed tea to the table, walked four short paces back to the kitchen, and returned with a couple of china teacups. She poured a cup first for me, and another for herself.

"Now, how may I be of assistance?" she said, sitting down in a rattan chair opposite me, crossing her legs. One flip-flop hung down off her heel.

I sipped the tea. It was hotter and stronger then I had expected of jasmine. "Thank you for allowing me up without proper notice," I smiled, placing the cup down. "I was hoping to speak with Mrs. Lawson."

Devon grinned. "Best to call her Virginia. Ginny if you know her well enough. But never Mrs. Lawson. She's not fond of the possessive connotation."

"Hmm. I must be showing my age. I thought today's women were happy to find Mr. Right."

"Mr. Centaur."

"Please, call me Jack." I said, feeling a sudden shame, hoping I didn't sound as if I was hitting on my host, instead of just being cordial.

"Jack," Loretta began again. "These American women can't wait to find Mr. Right. They promise him everything, and then as soon as he commits to a wedding date, they cross their legs and don't open up again until they want something."

I didn't like her comment about *these American women*. But I was also thinking that she wasn't completely wrong in her statement. "Well, certain type of women," I conceded.

"No, Jack. You're right. Don't mind me. I'm just a bit sensitive on the matter. I'm certain that your niece Candice was not that way."

"How well did you know Candice?"

"Not very," Devon shrugged. "I did see her occasionally at the clubs around town. Sometimes with Maria. Sometimes with another woman friend. And the one time, before the event, when she came here to try on the Fargo design she would be wearing."

"Your partner seemed to know my niece well."

"Not really. Just from Michael's office. Whenever she went up there to drive her husband loony."

"Not exactly the lovebirds, I gather."

Devon placed the teacup to her lips. Sizing me up as she drank. She lowered the cup and said, "One might come to that conclusion."

"How'd you wind up to be partners with her?"

"In London. Three years ago. My father had recently passed away. I was trying to save what was left of his agency."

"Your father had a modeling agency?"

"Talent." Loretta nodded to a bank of photographs mounted on the partition. Mostly, the usual Wall of Fame of photo opportunity shots taken at celeb bashes.

Devon pointed to an 8-by-10 glossy off by itself. It was taken in front of a club in the East End of London. The kind tourists never would dare frequent. I knew the place. I'd been there more than once.

The photograph showed a group of five men and one woman. All Middle Eastern. All I guessed to be in their twenties, except for the man at the far left, who stood wearing a stark white suit that contrasted with the dark night and the darkness of his skin. His black hair gleamed in the light given off by the flash. And he wore a broad smile, as if presenting the group to the world.

"That's my father in his white suit. Kind of his trademark."

"Like Tom Wolfe."

"Who?"

"Never mind. I'm showing my age again." I nodded towards the photograph. "Please, go on."

Devon looked at me with a bit of confusion and continued.

"I think the suit had something to do with a cover from a Beatles album. Anyway, he thought he was going to be the next Brian Epstein; only he'd be promoting Bollywood talent to the West.

"Your father was very handsome."

"Yes, he was."

"And your mother?"

"That's her in the middle. My mother." Devon couldn't help showing her resentment. I would have noticed the resemblance given a minute. It was so strong to that of the woman sitting across from me.

"Father made the cardinal sin of the business. He married a client. She was a rising rock singer in India. Father promoted her in London."

"Is she still in the business?"

"She's dead."

"I'm sorry."

"Don't be. She killed my father."

"Excuse me?"

"Well, not in the way the police arrest you for," Devon continued. "Mother," again with a tone of resentment, "had a heroin habit she had hidden from father for quite some time.

"She missed bookings. They fought. He tried to get her more gigs. But all he could do was get her into shitty, low-paying clubs. Father tried to get her a record deal. But by then, she was shooting up all the time. Refused to enter rehab. Eventually, AIDS did her in. And my father was never the same. It shattered him. He thought himself this big pitchman. Living in London his entire life. Believed he was so Western, but he had a lot of my grandfather's old world ways. His wife being a drug addict wasn't as much a sickness to Father as it was a family disgrace. He blamed himself. I found him dead in his flat. He had found my mother's stash and shot himself up with her heroin."

Devon took a final sip of tea and placed the cup down. "Sorry I got into this with you. Believe me I empathize with your loss."

"You still haven't told me how you came to be partners with Virginia?"

"I haven't, have I?" She said, throwing out another smile.

"Father didn't leave much of an estate. Only a few thousand pounds or so left after I paid for the burial expenses. I wasn't starving. I did have decent employment with a public relations firm in London. Yet, I was distraught. And I was lonely.

"I'm sitting at a local pub, crying in my beer, as you Americans call it, when I bumped into an old friend from university. She's with a bunch of people, one of whom was Ginny Kirk. Not yet married to Michael. You should know, Mr. Centaur, Virginia can be very endearing, when she wants to be."

"I wouldn't know."

"Well, you'll learn." Devon curled her lips. "So there in the pub, Virginia starts in trying to convince me how well I would do in New York. Says everyone in New York City loves a British accent. 'They'll just die to be able to *like* call you a friend' she tells me."

"She's right about that," I agreed.

"Well, I was ready for a change. So I took what money I had and crossed the pond, as they say."

Devon's cell phone rang. She looked at the caller ID.

"The rest is quite simple," she continued, letting the call go to voice mail. "Virginia Kirk worked her way from production assistant at Lawson Worldwide Media to Mrs. Michael Lawson. She had more social contacts than I would ever have. After all, she's been tossed from every private school in the city. But business-wise, she doesn't know a damn thing about being a publicist. What Ginny does have, though, are gonads."

"In this city that's what you need most."

"So I've learned."

"So she begins to feed you clients."

"Yes, and I do all the work."

"And Ginny does the partying."

"Yes, and before long she wants to be my partner."

"And you agree because you're new in town and she can make or break you."

"And she insisted her name is to go before mine on the stationery. I say why not alphabetically? 'Well, *like who has all the contacts?*' she whines."

"Did she bring in Fargo?"

"Yes."

"Has the Fashion Killer got it in for Fargo?" I asked, getting to where I'd been heading.

"Freshen your tea?" Devon asked, not shocked a bit by the directness of my question.

I declined her offer.

Devon continued, "Fargo's like most artists. A sweetheart when it's to his advantage to be so. And a completely irrational child when things don't go his way."

"And your job is to make sure the public only sees the sweetheart."

"At times, it's quite the job."

"I hear his ex-partners are not too fond of him."

"After the way he left them?"

"Oh?"

"About three years ago—"

"Around the same time you crossed the pond."

"Yes, I guess so," Devon shrugged. "Around three years ago, Fargo teamed up with Wayne and Nelka. They worked together, lived together and who knows what else they did together. But they did produce a new hip kind of fashion that appealed to the Upper Eastside trust-fund babies. Kind of gave them the feeling that they were the new 70's generation. A new kind of ME generation. Anyway, Fargo felt he no longer needed partners because, after all, so Fargo tells it, HE was the creative genius and Wayne and Nelka were just riding on his wave."

"Maybe one of the jilted partners hates seeing anyone wearing a Fargo."

"Maybe it's just Lawson models someone hates."

"My niece was not a Lawson model."

"Much to my partner's regret," Devon frowned. "Yet, your niece did attend the party at Michael's request. The killer could have thought she was a Lawson Girl."

"Is that what you think? It's not Fargo, but Lawson Worldwide someone wants to destroy?"

"Jack. I let you up here out of respect for your loss. And because Maria is my friend."

"Thank you, I appreciate you seeing me. But I need answers. I need to know why my niece was killed. You know, closure."

"I have the feeling it's more than closure you're after."

I found I had pushed myself forward to the edge of the rattan chair. I sensed I'd better ease off.

"I'm sorry," I said, sliding back. "It's just been difficult. I mean I just can't fathom why I lost her. That's all."

"Take it from one who knows," Devon offered, the tension gone from her voice, replaced by an understanding tone of someone who knows the futility of searching for unanswerable questions. "You need to get on with your life. No matter how void it might feel at the moment."

"Yes, I know you're right."

"I understand you purchased a table at the benefit dinner," Devon said, trying to change the direction of our conversation.

"Yes, Maria wants to go," I lied.

"I hope she enjoys herself."

"So maybe these trust-fund babies aren't all as bad as the gossip sheets say. I mean they do raise a lot of money for charity."

I wasn't sure that Devon was buying into my sudden respect for the altruism of the idle rich.

"Yes," Devon agreed. "Michael and Virginia are co-chairs of the Young Metropolitans League. And Lawson Worldwide purchases several tables at every event. I must say, though, that's pretty much the way with all the brood. Their parents are the biggest contributors. They buy tables and let the kids wallpaper the room by inviting celebs and wannabees free of charge. "

"And a driving publicist will make sure her clients are part of the wallpaper," I said.

"Get your client in Sunday Styles Section of *The New York Times* or Page Six of the *Post*. And especially into the blogs. You must get them into TMZ. That's the goal."

I was about to say, *Or maybe the front page of the Journal,* when the turn of a door bolt distracted me.

"Speak of the devil," Loretta Devon muttered.

TWELVE

WITH THE FORCE OF A hurricane, Virginia Kirk-Lawson stormed into the room. A Marc Jacobs shopping bag looped over her left forearm. A black leather portfolio in her right hand.

"Oh fuck that shit!"

I thought she was shouting at us, until I saw the Bluetooth stuck to the side of Virginia's head.

"The bitch owes me," she said, standing still in the center of the room, oblivious to anyone around her. A slice of sunlight caught her face at an angle giving her dark pupils the red-eye of a bad photograph. Her paunchy cheeks narrowed down into a long, pointed chin. She had brown hair, streaked with dyed red highlights. Her cut-off blouse exposed enough midriff that she could have been the "before" in a Weight Watchers ad. And the way her low-cut pants were pulled tightly across her hips, she should have been required by state law to paste a "wide-load" sign on her ass. Three weeks past Labor Day, and her skin was the nauseating brass-tone of a fading East Hampton tan.

"You'd better have a fuckin' six o'clock for me TODAY when I show up," she said, slapping off the Bluetooth with a chubby finger. "Can you believe?" Finally acknowledging her partner's presence. "My hair looks like shit, and that whore says she has nothing open until tomorrow." Then to me she said: "Who are you?"

I wondered how it happened that a good looking rich guy like Michael Lawson got stuck marrying a zaftig witch who possessed less class then an Eleventh Avenue hooker.

Devon gave me a what'd-I-tell-you look and said: "Jack Centaur, meet my partner, Virginia Kirk-Lawson. Virginia, Mr. Centaur is Candice's uncle."

I stood up. Offered my hand. When was I going to learn? The witch didn't offer hers back.

"What do you want here?" she quipped.

"Dropped by for a spot of tea," I replied, lowering my unnoticed hand. "Care to join us?"

Devon placed a delicate brown hand up to her mouth, suppressing a chuckle.

"You know, I would have made your niece famous."

I was glad she didn't bother to offer her condolences. I might have puked.

"So I've been told."

"She was very stubborn, your niece. Acted as if she didn't like money."

"Maybe she just didn't like what it does to some people," I repeated for the second time that morning onto deaf ears.

"Whatever," she said, then turned to Devon and said: "I have a four-thirty with Kim Ray. She's like totally fuckin' everything up."

"Kim's the coordinator of the gala," Devon was polite enough to inform her guest who was still standing, allowing a lady to be seated first. And then to Virginia she said: "Mr. Centaur has purchased a table."

The witch's toilet-lid upper lip exposed all gums when she smiled. The price she paid for her perfect white teeth probably cost more than the ten grand I had spent for the table. "How nice," she said. The words oozing from her mouth like KY Jelly.

"After all, the money is going for a good cause," I smiled.

Virginia Kirk-Lawson's face froze trying to recall just what cause it was she cared so much about. "Yes, yes of course. Your donation will buy lots of...of...important stuff." She turned to her partner.

"Yes, Mr. Centaur, the Pets Without Partners Fund is very thankful for your generous support," Devon said, saving her partner's ass. Which is what I expect she did most of the day.

"Yes…Yes! The poor things. Wonderful cause." Virginia smiled even wider. Then she rolled her eyes, directing her words again at Devon.

"Kim has no fucking clue what she's doing. She's going to fuck up the program. I'm sure of it. I told her the printer I wanted for the program and the bitch went to some schmuck downtown instead."

I cringed, hoping Smoothe Press wasn't that schmuck.

Virginia moved over to the business end of the glass table, placing the shopping bag on the floor. She pushed a stack of papers aside to make room for her Gucci brief case.

Still standing, she said, "As you can see, Mr. Centaur, I'm very busy. Is there a reason, other than tea, that you're here?"

"Seems everyone's having a busy morning, *Mrs. Lawson.*" I paused to enjoy the witch's nostrils flare red. "My niece was found dead in your suite. And I'd liked to know why."

"Go to the police."

"I did. And now I'm here."

"What the fuck for? I told them everything. Your niece had had it with the party. She said she was going home. She went to our suite to change. A maniac killed her. End of story."

"No, Mrs. Lawson. That's just *like* fucking part of the story where I came in. Now sit your fat ass down."

"You can't come in…" the witch began, thought better of it, and slowly lowered herself into the chair. "Okay, Mr. Centaur. Okay. I've been totally callous. You must be feeling like sooo awful. I'm sorry. Please, will you forgive me?"

From the corner of me eye I saw Devon turn her head away in disgust.

I did not bother to dignify the women's false sincerity. I said, "Who had access to your suite?"

"Just Michael and me."

"No one else used your room to change?"

"The only other people who entered the room were Fargo and a stylist. Turned out the stylist could have stayed at home. All Candice needed was a touch of makeup for effect. I mean, she had like sooo much natural beauty. I'm telling you I could have made her the next big thing."

I controlled my urge to reach across the table and choke Virginia's arrogant fat neck, and said, "You knew that this…this Fashion Killer was targeting Fargo models. How the hell could you let anyone into another dress of his?"

"Like Michael was like really concerned about the safety of your niece. He even provided a driver to take her home. The car was waiting out front. All I know is Michael gave her the key to our suite, and I fuckin' swear that was the last time I saw your niece." Virginia ran her plump fingers through her ratty hair. "I mean, like well, that is until I found her…her body in the bathroom."

I felt like a fool for not having asked Dent such an obvious question. *Who found the body?" Isn't that the first thing a real detective asks?* But I was no real detective. Just an angry relative of the victim, totally in over his head, bumbling his way through a maze of bullshit.

"You were the first to see my niece dead?"

"Yes, I found her. I thought you knew. Oh you can't imagine! I walked into the suite, took off my dress, went to pee, and there, right there in fuckin' front of me, on the floor, is a dead body. Oh my god! I couldn't even scream. I thought I was going to pee right there in my pants. It was like slow motion. All I could do was just about like grab my cell and call Michael. I'm not like even sure what I said to him. He was still down in the club, I think. Anyway he must have caught an elevator right away, he like got to the room so fast."

"What did he do?"

"He called his father's cell."

"What for?"

"Like what else should he have done?"

"How about LIKE calling 9-1-1? Maybe my niece was still alive. Maybe he could have gotten an ambulance."

"She was dead! She was dead! It was horrible. I'd never seen a dead person before." Virginia was again running the plump fingers through her hair.

"Michael tried to reach his father twice in, like, maybe four or five minutes and only got his voice mail. Then Michael called 9-1-1. I mean it couldn't have been more than...than ten, maybe fifteen minutes from the time I found her. I mean Michael just wanted to talk to his father. You can understand that. Can't you?"

Devon's cell phone rang. Once more she looked at the caller ID and let the call pass to voice mail.

"Who was that?" Virginia asked.

"Not important," Devon replied.

"What are you trying do, Mr. Centaur, make Candice's death MY fault?"

I had no idea what I was trying to do. I was grasping at straws. I just wanted something to click. To jump up and tell me the connection between these trust-fund brats and the Fashion Killer.

"One last thing," I said.

"Good," Virginia grunted. "What?"

"How long after Michael handed Candice the key did you go up to the suite?"

"I don't know. Maybe an hour. Maybe a drop more. You know, Mr. Centaur," the witch sighed. "It takes like forever to say good night at one of these fuckin' dinners."

THIRTEEN

THE BROOKLYN HEIGHTS SAVINGS BANK building is the kind of structure that makes people feel their money is safe. It's big, stone, and has been standing on the same spot on Henry Street for more than a hundred years.

And Betty Nolen was as much a fixture in the place as the gilded ceiling and marble-topped counters. About the only thing that looked out of place was the ATM in the vestibule where I now stood. It wasn't even a full month since she lost Candice, and I had thought maybe it was too soon to go back to work.

But Betty had insisted. "I can't be sitting around here any more," she had told me.

So my sister cleaned up the apartment, carted the garbage out to the street curb, slammed the trash can shut and swore out loud, "That son-of-bitch ain't going to kill me too." Then she squared her shoulders and headed straight off into the world again.

I managed a smile, seeing her come through the vestibule door. The dress she wore on her first day back wasn't black, but it was dark enough for a person in mourning.

"How'd things go?"

"Okay, I guess," she shrugged. "I'll just have to get used to the pity looks and all."

"Eventually they'll stop. People mean well."

"Did you see the beautiful flowers they sent to the chapel?"

"Very nice."

"And Bob and his wife coming to the wake and the funeral and all. And her due any minute."

"You always said for such a young man he's very mature."

"In thirty-three years I've sure seen lots of bosses come and go. They seem to be getting younger and younger all the time."

"Thirty-three years. Unbelievable! Where the hell has all the time gone, Betty?"

She slipped her arm through mine. We walked nestled together, not speaking, the whole five blocks to Montague Street.

The weather for the first Monday of October was still mild enough for the Heights Cafe to have sidewalk seating. Come the end of the month, the cool wind blowing in off the harbor would change that.

A young hostess picked up two menus, turned her back to us looking for an open table and saying, "I've got a deuce opening up. Take a sec to clean it."

We looked at the sidewalk tables filled with yuppies.

"Wasn't like this when we were kids, huh?" Betty said. "Street gangs and all."

"Ah, Brooklyn has it ups and downs, but it always comes back. It's in its nature to fix itself."

"Follow me," the hostess said, her back still to us. A busboy was placing setups down on a table for two near the perimeter railing that separated the sidewalk diners from the pedestrians. And from the smokers, who had to take their cancer sticks out onto the sidewalk because of the mayor's new no-smoking law.

"How many auditions do you think she's had this week?" Betty commented, as the young hostess walked back to her post.

"Who knows? Might see her on All My Children someday. She's cute enough."

"Put your eyes back in your head," my sister smirked.

A kid of a waiter, with too many tables to handle, burst up asking, "Something to drink?"

Betty ordered an iced tea.

"Corona, no lime, no glass," I said. "And we're in a rush."

"Tell me about it," the waiter shot back.

"We'll both have the Chef Salad."

"You got it."

The salads and the drinks came at the same time.

"You know she called me from the party," Betty said, staring down at her salad.

"What? Candice called you. You never told me this."

"It was no big deal. She always called to say she was on her way home. I'd never went to sleep until she called me."

"When… What time?"

"Letterman was doing his monologue. Twenty-to-twelve…quarter-to-twelve. I don't know," Betty shrugged. "Before midnight, that's for sure."

"What'd she say?"

"Nothing. Says she'll be home soon, her boss has a car waiting for her. Said she was calling me on her way up to his room to change."

"Why didn't you tell me this before?"

"I don't know. Jesus, Jack what's the matter with you?"

I was getting intense. Upsetting my sister. Yet, I couldn't help myself. "Just tell me what else Candy said."

"Said she hated the whole party. Called them all a bunch of spoiled selfish brats," Betty said, poking the air with her fork, her eyes narrowing into angry slits. "She just hoped that maybe that piece of shit wife of Michael would get the hell off her case now about modeling."

"She sure is a piece of shit."

"You've met her?"

"That morning a few weeks ago after my meeting with Detective Dent. Took all I had to keep from smacking the bitch." I took a deep swig of the Corona, then added, "But I can't say the same for when I met her husband, though."

"Jackie! You HIT Michael Lawson?"

"Forget about it. Just tell me what else Candy said?"

"You gotta be kiddin' me."

"It was no big deal. Really. It'll do the kid good. Come on, what else did Candy say?"

"Nothing. Girl talk. I was tired, y'know." Betty lowered her head to sip the iced tea, and then gazing up at me as if recalling something, added, "You know something, I'm pretty sure there was someone with her."

"What do you mean?"

"You know how a person sounds when they're talking to you on the phone while someone else is around. Their voice just sounds a little different. I can't explain it. Just different. Y'know what I mean?"

"Maybe she was calling from the elevator. Could be there were a few people around watching the floor lights blink by."

"Yeah, she was on the elevator, but she got off. She said so. Said this was her floor to me over the phone. Kind of like automatic. Natural, muttered something like, oh here's my floor. Whatever…but that's not what I'm talkin' about. It was something else. I just sensed she was walking with someone. Not a stranger. A friend. Someone she must have known. Oh, I don't know. Maybe I'm just going crazy. Maybe she *was* alone."

"Did you tell this to Dent?"

"Not about the feeling that she was with someone. Just that she called to say she was coming home." Then it hit Betty. The thought of what she had just said. Of why her brother was so intense. "Oh my God, Jackie! Do you think she was walking with The Fashion Killer?"

"I don't know. But you'd think that someone would have seen her get into the elevator."

"Jack, the police must have asked around. I mean, what it's they say on TV? Ah—routine questions. That's it."

Once again I wondered who the hell I thought I was, trying to play detective. At least, my sister watched cop shows. She didn't spend all her time reading financial statements, like her brother. I was seriously considering going to Barnes and Noble to see if there was such a book as A Schmuck's Guide to Being A Detective. Instead, I went to the bathroom to pass the Corona, and then fumbled through my wallet for his card, and called Dent.

"Hello Mr. Centaur," Dent said, answering the cell number on his business card.

"Too bad killers don't have caller ID."

"Eventually they do, Mr. Centaur. Eventually they do."

"Look, my sister just told me something you need to know. My niece called her from the hotel just before she was killed."

"Mrs. Nolen already told me this."

"Yeah, but she didn't tell you about having this feeling her daughter was not alone when she called her."

"Who does she think was with her?"

"Doesn't know. Doesn't even know for sure anyone was. Just a mother's hunch."

"Right now that might the best hunch we have."

"Well? Did anyone see her get into the elevator? I mean, you did question people," I said, trying to sound as if I knew that this was all routine stuff.

"Mr. Centaur, are you now in the investigation business?"

"Drop the mister shit. I don't like being patronized. You want me doing exactly what I'm doing. And I'm pretty sure I know why."

"Where are you?"

"Brooklyn Heights." I said, not bothering to mention the part about standing over a urinal.

"You just caught me leaving Police Plaza. Do you have time to meet with me?"

"When?"

"Now."

"I'll catch the Number 2 train. It will be faster than a cab."

"Okay, but don't meet me here. I'll meet you outside the Park Place Subway station."

I returned to the table and told Betty I had to go meet Dent.

"Come on, Jackie. What the hell are you doing? Give it a break. We're never going to find who killed her. I want to move on. Please."

"I can't move on yet. I need to do this. I have reasons you'll never understand. No one will ever understand but me."

"You think I don't know? When they're dead, they're dead, Jackie. You can't bring anyone back. Let them rest in peace."

"*They* are resting in peace. It's me who's not."

I slipped Betty a hundred, and told her to make sure she gave the cute hostess a twenty for cab fare to her next cattle call.

"You just love throwing this stuff around, don't you?"

I bent down and kissed Betty's cheek. "Call it an investment in the arts," I said, and rushed off to catch the subway to Manhattan.

FOURTEEN

THE NUMBER 2 SUBWAY TRAIN takes less than fifteen minutes to travel from Clark Street to Park Place. From soothing, tree-lined streets to the hurried bustle of the downtown center of the world's biggest metropolis. From residential brownstones to the monolithic pillars of justice, all in only three quick subway stops.

Within the shadows of City Hall, Court Houses, and Police Plaza stood Detective Jim Dent, waiting at the top of the stairwell as I climbed the gritty, concrete steps up to the street.

Dent's black suit, white shirt and dark tie, were as fresh and crisp as they had been on that morning we had met at the precinct—his handshake just as firm.

"Have you had lunch?"

"Yes," I said.

"Well, I haven't."

We walked to the curb. Stood under the umbrella of a street vendor's cart. Dent got a meat kabob and a Diet Coke. Handed the thin, little Middle-Eastern vendor a ten, pocketed the change and said, "Let's go."

He wolfed down the beef cubes straight off the toothpick-skewer like a man used to eating on the run.

BY THE TIME we reached the corner of the block, Dent was wiping his mouth with a tiny white napkin. He tossed the napkin and the skewer into a NYC Department of Sanitation trash basket. He kept the Diet Coke.

We walked side by side, both of us with just enough of a telltale hard-guy bopping stride still left in our steps to prove we had both grown up on the tough New York City streets.

"How's your sister holding together?"

"She's strong, in public," I said. "It's when she's alone in her apartment, that I'm not sure of."

"She's going to need to move out of her place. Every time she looks around she must see something that reminds her of her daughter."

"My sister is not made that way. That apartment is her home. Always has been. She didn't leave it after her husband died, and she won't let this killer push her out now."

"I get the feeling the Centaurs don't take to being pushed around."

We were not walking in any particular direction, but perhaps it was the frustration with the way things were going in the investigation that we wound up at Vessey Street. We stopped, staring in silence out over the vast open space that tourists called Ground Zero, and the city's inhabitants still called The World Trade Center.

"What happened here pisses everyone off," Dent began again. "But to a guy who has fought for his country it must really hit hard."

"Stings like hell," I said.

Dent remained staring out at the void and said, "My father died in Nam."

I turned to look at Dent's face.

I never ask how a man died in Vietnam. If someone needs to tell me, that's okay; if not, that's okay, too. The fact was Dent's father didn't make it home. And that was all *I* needed to know.

"You must have been very young."

Dent took a last quick sip of his Coke, crushed the can and tossed it into a nearby construction dumpster. He then turned and faced me straight on. "I was seven years old," he said. "My father died on the last damn day of the war. He was a chopper pilot, pulling escaping Vietnamese civilians off a roof in Saigon. The chopper so full it couldn't handle the weight. Crashed. No one survived."

I began speaking now as if I had somehow just swung open a long-shut closet door stuffed with old familiar tools. Jungle jargon I had not uttered in years sprang from my mouth.

"Chopper pilots had the respect of every grunt humping in the boonies," I said. "Hovering over a hot LZ, waiting for us grunts to board, made their Hueys sitting ducks for Charlie's rocket grenades. Rumor was, any Charlie brought down a Huey got a week's R&R in Hanoi."

"My old man did two tours."

"So you didn't see him since you were three?"

"He came home for a few weeks between tours. We lived in a small apartment complex off-base, in Wrightstown, New Jersey."

"I spent the last few months before my discharge at Fort Dix. Assigned to the Five-Thirty-Second Military Police Company."

"Stateside, you were an MP?"

"Nah, I caught a break for a change. All I did was pound a typewriter for six months, processing court-marshaled soldiers into the stockade. Never even carried a weapon."

"So you know that Wrightstown, sandwiched right there between Fort Dix and McGuire Airbase, was a real military town. Probably still is. I haven't been back since Mom and me moved to Queens to live with her sister after dad was buried.

"Your dad was a lifer?"

"No, he wasn't going to make a career of the Army. Mom said he pulled a low lottery number and got drafted right after graduating college. And somewhere along the way he opted for helicopter school."

"That automatically made him a warrant officer when he graduated," I said, remembering getting the same carrot dangled in front me right after basic training and turning it down.

"And that stuck him with a four-year commitment, instead of the two draftees had," Dent smirked. "Anyway, he comes home for those few weeks, but tells me he's going to have to go back. Just for a little while. The war is ending, he says, and he wants to help bring the guys home."

I listened, and thought of how Dent had only known his father for a short time, yet he spoke of the man with the passion of a lifetime of loving. Candice sometimes spoke the same way about her dad. But, she could only remember him from photographs Betty always showed her.

"My father took me for a walk through the Pine Barrens the morning just before he was to leave," Dent said. "Early March '75. I can still see the chill of his breath as he spoke. He held my hand. I may have been only seven at the time, but I can still remember that morning as if it was yesterday, the planes from the airbase cutting the sky above us. You know something, my father could rap off the name of every aircraft just from the sound of its engine. He didn't even have to look up half the time.

"I had on a child's size fur-lined flight jacket, just like the one my father was wearing. Still have it. My son wears it now, sometimes." Dent turned back to face Ground Zero. "I tried not to show my dad I was cold, you know, didn't want him to think I wasn't tough, but even with the jacket on, my teeth chattered. So he pulls me in close to his side, looks down at me and says, 'Son, there are things left undone I need to help finish. When I'm through I'll be home.'

"I can still hear my words to him. 'Dad, when you get back, you gonna stay home for good?' 'Sure will,' he promised. Then he lifted me up into his arms and carried me back to the car. I've never felt warmer in my life. It was as if the man generated heat. Anyway, I never saw him again after that morning."

Dent now turned to face me again, his eyes filled with anger.

"What the hell had he left undone? Why'd he think HE had to go back to pull people out? One chopper more or less wasn't going to make a difference in the outcome of that war."

I had come to this meeting for my own purposes. I had no desire to become friends with a cop. What the hell did this cop think? I didn't have a clue about what another man's inner ghost might be. I had enough of my own ghosts to deal with.

Yet, I knew I owed Dent's father something. Something that had nothing to do with being this cop's friend.

"Maybe, maybe, he just had to be there to see how it all ended," I said. "Maybe he felt that was the only way he could finally figure out why we were in Nam in the first place. An awful lot of Vietnam Vets are still trying to work that one out. Maybe what was left undone was only in his mind. Maybe it only had to make sense to him."

We stood silent for a few minutes, both lost in our own pasts.

Dent was the first to come back to the present. "You're not going to stop until you find the Fashion Killer, are you?"

"Call it my second tour of duty," I grunted.

"It didn't do my father any good."

"You don't know that, do you? Detective, some things are worth dying for."

"That Medal of Honor—"

"I told you it was a mistake."

"My father got a posthumous one."

This time Dent had thrown me I curve I hadn't seen coming. I paused, then said, "Your father deserved his."

"I don't know what ghosts haunt you—"

"That's not any of your concern," I said, abruptly cutting the man off.

Dent hesitated for a long beat, then said: "I've been on the job fifteen years, and in all that time I have never broken a rule. Hardly even bent one. Now you're asking me to risk those years by helping you, a vigilante."

"A Medal of Honor winner," I said, using the award as a wedge, now understanding why the detective had let the conversation go this far.

Dent turned to face the crater once more, then turned again to face me. With the slow rhythm of a man laying out the rules of a game he wanted to remain in control of said, "The society crowd is your kind of people."

"In some ways I'm as much of an outsider as you are," I advised the man who I had just succeeding in pulling to my side of the court. "They play with blueblood money. I play with street money."

"But you've the bread to buy your way in."

"Only so far. They'll let me donate money to some pet cause, but if I want to join one of their clubs, they'll take a long look down their old-money noses at me."

"You ever wonder why it is that any bad light that might shine on them is reflected away?" Dent smirked. "It's because they live in houses made of mirrors. And I'm sure a man with your war record will use whatever means necessary to smash those mirrors to get what he's after."

I figured I knew where Dent was heading so why not help the guy along. "I've already purchased a table for Lawson's next benefit dinner."

The detective shook his head. "You move fast."

I unfolded my crazy plan to smash the mirrored walls, using Maria as my gateway into the brat pack. Then I told the detective of my meetings with Loretta and Virginia. I left out the part about roughing up the Lawson kid.

"Michael Lawson is hiding something," I said. "He got up to the suite in nothing flat according to his wife. And I don't buy he may have caught the express elevator. He rushes up then decides to call his old man before calling 9-1-1."

It was now Dent's turn to offer up information.

"Didn't matter. We were already on our way by the time Michael called. Got our call four minutes before we got his."

"Our call?"

"We get a call right after each murder. Tells us exactly where to find the body. And the caller doesn't bother calling 9-1-1. The call comes directly into the precinct. My precinct."

"You trace it, right? Or whatever the hell it is the police do electronically these days."

"If it came from a cell phone, even a disposable one, we'd have something to go on. But the calls come from random phone booths. We've gone over each booth with a fine-tooth comb. Nothing. Whoever does the calling probably wears surgical gloves. Not that it matters much. It's impossible to find a good print on a public phone."

"What about the voice. I mean, aren't your calls recorded? Can't you analyze the voice? Get something to go on from that?"

"Yeah we automatically record 'em." Only the killer's voices are synthetic. You know, the kind you invoke on a word processor to read back text aloud."

"Voices?"

"The first victim, a female voice; the second and third murder a male voice; and your niece's again in a female voice."

"So you've got nothing."

"Nothing, except that our tech people have determined that whoever is making the calls is using some kind of iPod or MP-3 player."

"Great. Just stop and question every person in the city wearing earphones."

"I'll tell you one thing, I think your sister is right about someone your niece knew being with her."

"Why?"

"Because with none of the murders has there been a forced entry. Everything at the crime scene is neat and in order. Whoever it is gets close enough to commit the murder without any signs of a struggle."

I listened, my teeth grinding against my tongue so hard I could taste my own blood. *She knew the bastard.*

"Yes, I need someone like you on the inside," Dent said. "I need you to be my eyes and ears with these so-called pillars of society. And in turn, I'll keep you informed. Strictly off the record, of course."

"But you don't want me to go in for the kill," I managed saying through my clenched teeth.

"Not unless it's self-defense. If it's an execution," Dent said, his eyes latching hard onto mine, "I will arrest you for murder."

"Self-defense, huh?"

"Centaur, you have to promise me if you come up with anything. Anything! You'll call me. We'll go in together."

I opened my mouth just enough to get the words out. Just enough for Dent to see the red blood seeping through the spaces between my white teeth.

"I promise you this," I said. "I'll call you if I think you've got a better shot at killing the bastard."

Dent took a deep breath, hesitated, then said, "Candice made two calls before she called her mother."

"Yeah."

"One was to a girlfriend. A Jessica Nevin."

"Never heard of her."

"Nevin got the call in front of witnesses. She said Candice just called because she was bored. Was having a lousy time."

"Okay."

"The second person she called didn't pick up. And Candice hung up before the call went to voice mail."

"Another girlfriend?"

"No. Andy Smoothe."

"Did you question him about it?"

"Your partner is not one to answer questions much."

"Depends on who's doing the asking."

"Mr. Smoothe only confirmed that his cell phone showed a missed call from her number at about 10:15 PM. He couldn't guess as to why she would have been calling him."

"Then that's that. End of subject."

Dent straightened to his full height of six feet.

"Strange, don't you think," he said, tugging down the stiff sleeve cuffs of his starched shirt, until they extended neatly out an inch from his jacket sleeves.

"What?"

"That Candice called, her mother, her girlfriend, your partner, everyone that night except her *Uncle Jack*. The one name important enough to be written on the emergency card in her purse."

I didn't reply. It was none of Dent's damn business Candice had stopped speaking to her *Uncle Jack* three days before she was murdered.

FIFTEEN

A NOVEMBER DRIZZLE FELL ON the city. I entered the Museum of Modern American Art, rode the escalator up two floors to the Jackson Pollock Room, checked my Burberry with some dizzy blond staffer, and waited for Maria to arrive. I had sent a limo for her, but no orchid corsage—she was not my prom date. This was strictly business.

I was having problems seeing myself as the Sugar Daddy. I wasn't happy I'd have to pretend affection this evening to a woman who, as the cliché goes, was "young enough to be my daughter." I called it business. I called it role-playing. Whatever I called it, I still felt dirty. But I'd become Machiavellian in my quest to find The Fashion Killer, and knew very well that by the time it all came to an end, I'd be feeling a lot dirtier. So be it.

The Young Metropolitans paraded off the escalator onto a long red carpet. The invitation said they had come to help the homeless pets of East Hampton. Their swank said they had come to be seen in the Style Section.

A sprinkling of young men dressed in black tie. More dressed in an odd lot of jackets and torn jeans. Jackets and slacks. Some wore their tuxedos with Skechers and no socks. The women wore an eclectic array of gowns and miniskirts, slacks and designer T-shirts.

Watching it all, I marveled at how clever B.P. had been, to work crowds like this all those years with such perfection, with class, never losing her perspective. Sure, she had smiled broadly and kissed cheeks.

But she never bowed. "It's really very simple, Jackie," she once told me. "Don't ever for a minute believe your own bullshit."

And now here I was deep into my own world of bullshit, grasping for answers. If I could only determine the *why* someone would want to kill these young women then maybe I could figure out the *who* part.

I stood doubting the wisdom of my half-baked plan when I caught sight of Maria's face rising above the horizon of the escalator. First her face, then the broad shoulders, then her strong, shapely legs. She stepped from the escalator onto the red carpet. The show was about to begin. She wore a waist-length black leather jacket, a taffeta skirt under a ballerina-like tutu, and knee-high black leather stiletto-heeled boots. I walked over to greet my date. She rose up on her toes, and by some reflex, I found I had lowered my face, tasting her gentle kiss.

Our lips parted. Dazed, I helped Maria out of the jacket. Her shoulders were bare. A black silk halter-top rose up from beneath the taffeta top of her strapless dress. Her long muscular arms, bare. I handed the jacket to a waiting staffer who placed a coat-check into my palm. Like a breath of fresh air blown into a stale room, I inhaled the fragrance of Maria's perfume. A single rain droplet glistened on her forehead like a princess' diamond.

Removing a white handkerchief from my tuxedo jacket, I nodded. Maria gave me that smile of hers.

I patted away the diamond, and escorted my princess into the ballroom.

It was a night for gambling. A sea of green velvet casino tables made up the front half of the ballroom. Beyond the tables, a huge disco ball hung over a dance floor. A semicircle of dinner tables surrounded the dance floor. A thirty-piece swing band wailed from a stage.

If you want try your luck at casino gambling in the state of New York, head for an Indian reservation. Since Manhattan lost that status the minute the Manate tribe got trumped out of the island for twenty-four bucks in trinkets, I headed for the cashier's table where guests exchanged real dough for play money. Later, in the lobby, the same staffers who took the guests' coats to the checkroom will be standing behind glass display cases filled with useless crap donated by vendors of every kind.

Guests will peruse the counters, flaunting their winnings with fists full of colorful play money, buying things they'll forget in the limo on the way home. Come morning they'll warm themselves to the fire of their generosity, knowing they had given to a worthy cause. So what if they couldn't remember exactly what that cause might have been.

P-Cap and Mr. Coors Light, with his arm around her waist, stood ahead of us in the cashier's line. She was slipping a Platinum Visa back into her Prada purse, while holding a wad of play money. Mr. Coors Light was trying to slip his hand down from her waist. P-Cap wasn't letting him. When they left, I held out for the cashier, a thin, gray-haired man with hollow cheeks and a Socratic nose, a thousand in cash and said, "Pop, I thought you were going to spend your retirement sunning at Belmont."

Pop Wallace looked at the face attached to the hand holding the grand, and his thin red lips turned up at the corners.

"Jack! You old dog. How the hell ya doin'?"

"Been better," I said.

As if he had just told a dirty joke at an inappropriate time, Pop swallowed his smile. His face blushed, making the capillaries in his nose turn dark purple. "I'm sorry. Real sorry. I read your name in the paper and all. I should'a sent you a card. But ya know I ain't seen ya in years."

"Forget about it," I said, as he took the grand from my hand. "You'll always be okay with me, Pop."

"Was she…I mean, if you don't mind me asking. Was she…the one in the papers…was she the little girl used ta' carry the *Racing Form* for ya?"

"Yeah. My niece had a real knack for picking long shots."

"Ahh," Pop said, shaking his head with regret. "I shoulda sent a card or somethin'."

"So how come you're here?" I asked, in a hurry to change the subject.

"My wife passed. I couldn't sit home no more. She used ta' do charity work. So I figured I give it a shot."

Pop handed me my thousand dollars of the toy money.

"Well this is sure right up your alley," I laughed. For twenty years, Pop Wallace cashiered at the off-track betting office just down the block from Smoothe Press.

Now, for the first time, Pop took notice of Maria standing next to his old friend. "So...a...you're lookin' good these days," he said, his mouth crooking into a devious smile.

I folded the play dough.

"It's been good seeing you, Pop," I said, walking away with Maria, feeling Pop's eyes burning into back of my neck.

I had no trouble finding the table with the most action. The roar from the crapshooters ebbed like the rolling tide with every toss of the holy cubes.

"Whose the Asian fairy next to P-Cap and Mr. Coors Light?"

Maria rolled her eyes and jabbed her elbow into my ribs. "That's Benny Wang," she said.

I rolled my eyes. Maria sneered at me.

So we nestled up to the table squeezing in between P-Cap and Benny Wang and I laid the entire grand on boxcars and the red-headed dyke from Club Faux Pas threw double-six. The stickman pushed twelve grand worth of neatly stacked chips in front of me.

But I wanted more than a stack of chips; I wanted the attention of the crowd. And I got it. With every winning pass of dice, Maria, playing her role well, bounced childishly at my side. By the time the cubes made their way around the table into my fist, the pile of chips in front of me had grown to more than thirty grand.

I held the dice up for Maria to blow on for luck. She kissed them instead, her lips brushing against my fingertips.

I rolled a seven. Benny Wang squealed so high I thought his ass would burst out of his satin fuchsia pants.

More chips came my way.

I had reached a level of obnoxiousness that drew the brat pack to me like one of their own. They cheered my every move. These kids didn't get it. The charity only wins if the players keep returning to Pop to exchange their real bucks for play money. The kids were betting heavy on me, and I keep making passes. And as long as I kept rolling good numbers, Pop was going to be a lonely man.

Only the redheaded dyke was betting against me. She finally left without a chip, her blue eyes shooting out at me from under thin-penciled red eyebrows like a bullet filled with disdain. Right then I couldn't care less about being philanthropic. I needed these brats in my corner and the sheer, classless audacity of flaunting the money and groping Maria seemed to have put them into a Svengali trance.

"Can I get a little help with this load?" I said to the sea of young faces pressed three-deep against the sidewalls of the crap table. Wang was the first to grab a stack of chips. Then within a swell of accolades, more arms stretched across the table, scooping up chips.

"Sweeeet," someone said.

"You've got some pair of balls," a female voice squealed.

Wang giggled.

Then like the fading tide, the voices rolled quiet as the sea slowly parted.

We were equal in height, both just pushing the topside of six feet. From the tabloids, I knew we'd both been on the planet for the same number of years: fifty-six. While my thick, black Greek hair was sprinkled with the white salt of middle age, Bradford Lawson's colorist had kept his comb-over the same dirty blond it was when he first stepped out from the shadow of his aging father's construction business and into the limelight of the New York City real estate world.

It was a good deal turned brilliant by the thing that turns most deals brilliant: luck. The old man, Henry "Hank" Lawson, was born and bred on the conservative North Shore of Long Island, where the Depression of the 1930's never arrived. The green light Jay Gatsby envied from across the bay may very well have hung from the dock of the Lawson Estate.

Sometime during the Depression, the Lawson family picked up at auction a city block of near-empty factory buildings in the garment district. When the war came, prosperity returned, and once again the buildings were filled with clothing manufacturers. Up until the early 1980's, and the stampede of manufacturing to third world sweatshops, the Lawson family had collected hefty rents.

By 1988, the buildings were near empty again. So Hank says to his playboy son, show me what you can do, make something of these worthless buildings.

Timing is everything. In 1989 the Japanese once again attacked the United States. Only this time, instead of using planes, they attacked with money. Buying up everything they could put their hands on. So Bradford Lawson sold the empty buildings for top dollar to a group of Japanese investors, who then hired the Lawson Construction Company to convert the entire block from factory lofts to office suites.

Since the conservative Hank was never a leverage player, the buildings were debt free. With mortgage interest rates in the double-digit time bomb range, Bradford offered the new owners two percentage points below the market rate. Now the Japanese owned the property, and Lawson held the mortgage.

The mid-1990's the time bomb exploded. The Japanese investors were drowning in the debt of their buying spree. When they couldn't make the mortgage payments, Bradford foreclosed. Then went bragging it was his plan all along to set the foreign investors up for the fall. *Only he, Bradford Lawson, had the "savvy" to have seen the recession coming five years before anyone else.*

Then Lawson went on the buying spree, branding the family name on everything in Manhattan from office buildings to luxury apartments. If the Lawson name is on something, it had to be the biggest and the best.

So now what stood across the crap table from me was probably the most highly leveraged person in the country. Whatever Lawson owned was so mortgaged to the hilt that every banker in the city woke up in the morning, checked the obituary section of *The New*

York Times, and breathed a sigh of relief when they did not see Bradford Lawson's shit-eating grin plastered across it.

"I'll have my P.A. cash you in," Bradford Lawson said.

As if a silent command had been given to a pack of puppies, the arms of the Brat Pack reached again over the rail and placed the chips back onto the green felt.

"Have your *personal assistant* spread it out among the volunteer staffers outside to spend at the counters."

"Nice gesture," Bradford said, signaling to some flunky who took the chips away.

"Oh," I grinned. "Let me know how much it all comes to."

"Why? It's not real."

"I like to keep score." I said, walking away with Maria, giving her a little pat on the ass that I knew everyone would see.

This time Maria did get her boss onto the dance floor. Her moves were like a pole dancer. Mine were like the pole. As she swung about, an uneasy feeling I had gotten when helping Maria off with her coat returned. Then I had thought that it was just my nerves telling me how stupid my plan was. Now I knew it was something else. Her outfit!

I'd never before really seen Maria all dressed up. At Smoothe Press every day was casual day. Except for me. I had wallowed in sweat-drenched fatigues for too long not to want the feel of the best material money could buy against my skin.

I continued the old fart show while my posse from the crap table slithered onto the dance floor. As I turned about, my hands up in the air, trying to redeem something from my youth that might resemble dancing, I saw a few more women wearing outfits similar to Maria's. I stopped dancing. I grabbed my date's arm.

Maria flinched. "What's wrong?"

"Where the hell did you get this dress?" I shouted over the blaring music.

"Loretta."

"It's a Fargo!" I said, squeezing her arm

"I know. Let me go!"

I released my grip.

Rubbing her arm, Maria scowled. "I need to use the ladies' room."

I followed her off the dance floor.

Outside the ballroom, I checked her arm. It was red. I let out a deep aggravated breath and said, "You okay?"

"I'm fine," Maria said in a way I knew meant I had crossed a line.

I began to apologize. Maria brushed it off. We both knew I would never touch her that way again.

"How could you wear a Fargo?"

"I could never afford one of these," she said, fingering the fabric. "What the hell? Loretta offered to lend me it for tonight."

"Don't con me. It was more like you asked her for it. And I'll bet she didn't want to give it to you."

"Look around. I'm not the only one wearing a Fargo. These frickin' rich bitches all gotta have whatever's hot."

Only in the bizarre world of celebutants with bottomless checkbooks and credit cards without limits would the fashion statement of the moment be the thrill of wearing what may very well turn out to be their shroud.

"Yeah," I said, looking at the crowd. "It's like to die for."

Maria's lips twisted into a smirk. She started past me for the ladies' room. "I gotta pee."

"Forget about it. I'm not letting you out of my sight."

"Whadaya kiddin' me? I gotta go."

I whipped out my cell and hit speed dial. The phone hooked to my date's purse played a musical tone. She snapped it open with another smirk.

"Just keep talking," I said.

"Un-fuckin-believable."

I watched her walk through the ladies' room door and heard in my ear, "Hey wise-ass. How ya expect me to wash my hands?"

"Speakerphone!" I suggested.

"Un-fuckin-believable!"

SIXTEEN

I HAD SWORN I WOULDN'T put Maria in harm's way. But she proved
to have bigger balls than most men I know. She had dressed herself
up in a Fargo hoping to lure The Fashion Killer. And I didn't like
it. Didn't like it at all. Yet, I couldn't call it quits. Couldn't find it in
myself to do the smart thing and say, "Game over." I decided to play
it out. Maybe I'd catch someone staring at my date just a tad more
then they should be. Problem was Maria had the kind of body that
inspired long looks. Even from women. How was I going to separate
the lecherous and envious stares from the murdering kind?

I needed more eyes.

I thought of calling Dent. Getting him down there as a last-
minute guest. But ditched that idea, figuring the killer would spot a
cop hanging around. It was time to call my backup.

ANDY SHOWED UP fast. And all six-foot-five of him was pissed off. The
sight of him in a black tuxedo, black shirt and long black tie, together
with his dark eyes and thick black hair, was like the presence of the
grim reaper approaching me.

"You son-of-a-bitch, where is she?"

I swallowed hard, tried to speak, but could not come up with
anything but a nod in the direction of where Maria stood with a
tall, bulimic blond woman, and the same short, chubby brunette
I recognized from my night at Club Faux Pa. It looked as though

they might be comparing their Fargo designs. All three wore black.

"Don't fuckin' move," Andy said.

I stayed put, watching my partner march across the room.

As if the warning tremor of an earthquake was coming down upon her, Maria twisted her left shoulder back. The champagne flute she was about to sip from paused on her lips, her eyes widening above its thin rim. Fear was plastered across her face like the Ace of Spades on a cold deck.

She remained fixed that way, even when I could see Andy had already slipped into his charm mode. After a few chuckles from the chubette, and a blushing smile from the blond, Andy made a gentlemanly parting motion to the ladies and escorted the still dumbstruck Maria away.

His back to me, Andy stood with his broad shoulders hunched over Maria. From where I stood like an obedient dog, I could only imagine Andy's admonishments. At one point Maria's body language suggested she was about to rebuff her boss, when all the big guy did was tilt his head a half-notch to get the point across that she'd best not give him any flack.

When Andy finished reading Maria the riot act he led her by the hand back to her date.

"Now what, shamus?" he mocked.

"Look," I said, attempting a reconnaissance plan of sorts. "I'm going to nuzzle up to the fuchsia wang-wacker over there."

Maria had finally had it with me. "Will you stop with that homophobic shit already?" she snapped. "Hasn't it gotten you into enough trouble?"

My face must have gone blank.

Andy grimaced.

Maria, knowing she hit a nerve, sorry the words had ever left her mouth, added, "Look, Benny's a good guy. Really."

I owed Maria big-time, and rolled with the punch, saying to Andy, "Look, Maria will take you around and point out the women wearing Fargos."

"And what am I supposed to do, partner? Round 'em up like horses and shove them all into a corner."

"Uh...Watch out for anyone looking suspicious," I said.

Andy rolled his eyes.

I shook my head, walking over to where the plump little fire-plug stood with his big ass sticking out like a wide receiver waiting for a touchdown pass. I wouldn't know a Pink Martini from a Cosmopolitan, but I figured whatever drink it was Benny Wang had dangling from his three-fingered,-pinky-up grip, he chose it to match the gay little number he was wearing.

"What's that you're drinking?"

Benny Wang looked back over his shoulder with a who-the-fuck-wants-to-know attitude that suddenly lit up into a smile.

"Get out of town! If it isn't Mr. Seven-Eleven."

"I didn't know they had any in this city," I said, referring to the convenience store, not the dice.

"So whadaya want?" Benny shrugged. "I grew up in Joirzee."

"I won't hold it against you."

"Oh that's such a shame. I'm like sooo into older men."

"And I'm like sooo into Maria," I smirked.

"I'll bet you are." Benny said, waving his glass. Then he took a long, studying nod that traveled down to my toes, and back up to my face again. When he was done Benny said, "Pink Martini."

I must have looked confused.

Wang wiggled his glass. "The drink."

A waiter passed with a tray. Benny placed his drink on it. "I think maybe you'd prefer something more of your own world," he said, leading me off to the bar stand.

I ordered a Chivas, and to my amazement, so did Benny Wang.

Wang clanged his glass against mine. "You showed big balls blowing off Bradford Lawson like that."

"He's a pompous ass."

Benny swigged down the scotch with one swallow. He blotted his mouth with a napkin the way a woman does when she's wearing lipstick. "You did a pretty good job imitating one yourself."

"Are you saying I'm pompous, or just a phony?"

"Maybe both." Benny placed the empty tumbler down on the bar. "You're playing some kind of a game, Mr. Centaur."

I guessed Wang for no more than thirty-two. Yet, he had maturity on his face that seeped through its Botox facade. Minutes before he was nursing a pink, girly drink. Now the guy's belting down the hard stuff like it was milk. I knew first hand, only someone who has wallowed in some bad shit drinks that way.

"Yeah, I'm playing tag," I said. "I just don't know who's it yet."

"And the "it" murdered your niece."

I downed my scotch in one swallow and placed the empty tumbler down next to Benny's.

"And what game are you playing, Benjamin?"

A twinkle came into Benny Wang's eyes. "My mother used to call me Benjamin."

I gave Benny a look that said, I'm not your mother, and make your point.

Benny shrugged. "Candice was not having a good time that night."

"You were there?"

"Of course. I'm at all the events. I'm a charity whore."

"Then the police must have questioned you after each murder."

"Yes, they did. So what?"

"Come on, you're at every event. You didn't notice anything out of the ordinary? Nothing?"

"Are you kidding me? It's always the same assholes at these parties. The faces never change. Gets really totally fucking boring after a while."

"So it must be your philanthropic streak that brings you out,"

"Oh, paleeze. I told you, I'm a charity whore. I never pay."

"I should have guessed. You dress like wallpaper."

"You like?" Benny made a half-twirl.

"Beautiful."

"Mr. Centaur, I liked Candice." Benny frowned toward the crowd. "And I was about the only one."

"So what made my niece so special to you?"

"You know how it is when you meet someone you like instantly. It feels as though you've been friends in another life. You just hit it off so well."

I nodded. "Yes. Once. When I was seventeen."

"Well, that's how it was with Candice and me. We'd met that night for the first time and I already felt as though we were best friends. She didn't put on any act. She didn't play the gay game. That's what most people do, you know. Oh yeah. We're like toys. The young, hip straights, smile toting you around like you're their own personal gay trophy. *Look at me I'm not afraid of queers.*

"And believe me it doesn't just happen with the straights. Oh no. Gays play the game with each other. They decide whether they should be bitchy to you, or if they should fuck you, or maybe, really just be your friend.

"But with Candice it wasn't that way at all. She didn't like the people at the party and she told me straight out. I told her I didn't either. But, I said, at least it's a night away from my apartment."

Benny sighed. "And then the next day, without any warning, I'm walking over to get my bagel and cream cheese—the way I do every morning—and there hanging from a newsstand is that awful picture on the front page. I cried right there in the street, Mr. Centaur. I had made a friend. She'd given me her cell number and everything. And now she was gone."

"So you were two lonely, single gays out that night," I said. "Only what could you do? You like boys, and she went for girls."

Benny smirked and said, "And of course there's another player in the gay game. The straight player like you, Mr. Centaur, who just doesn't get it. You don't hate us. You don't even have disdain for us. You just throw your hands up and say, 'What a waste.'"

Benny had sized me up just right. And had the balls to tell me so. Yes, this was the kind of person Candice would have called a friend.

"So how come you two didn't leave together if you were so friendly and so bored?"

Benny shrugged. "Actually, that night, I did want to go someplace else with Candice. You know, just for coffee or something. But she was tired. She just wanted to get back home to Brooklyn. Said her boss had hired a car service to take her home. And then she went up to change out of that god-awful outfit she was forced to wear."

"Did you see her go into the elevator? I mean, was she alone?"

"She was alone. I walked her to the elevator. That's when she gave me her cell number. Told me to call her the next day. We'd get that cup of coffee after work."

"You're positive no one was in the elevator? I mean, when she got in? No one was already inside?"

"Mr. Centaur. There was no one. I'm positive."

"Benny, she called her mother on the ride up to the room. Her mother had this feeling someone was with her."

"Mr. Centaur I wish there was someone with her. Me! Maybe then she'd still be alive."

"Forget about it, Benny. Take my word, it doesn't work that way."

"I lost a friend before she ever really became one. And I feel helpless."

For a know-nothing sleuth, I was beginning to build up a nice little gang of operatives. I already had a frustrated cop, a hardheaded Brooklyn girl pretending to be my lover, a business partner who was getting more irritated with me by the minute, and now I was about to sign up a gutsy little man who dressed in fuchsia.

"Benny, you can help me. Maybe better than anyone else."

"How? How? Just tell me how."

I grinned. "How about treating me like I'm a real asshole homophobe. That shouldn't be too hard for you to do."

Benny grinned back. "That will be a no-brainer. But why?"

"You're going to be my inside man. I need the people around you to figure you can't stand me. Just maybe then someone might let something slip that they wouldn't if they thought we were friends."

I signaled the bartender for two more drinks. She poured them straight up and laid them on the bar-stand.

Benny and I reached for the tumblers at the same time. Then, with my free hand close to his hip, I slipped my business card into Benny's pants pocket.

Suddenly, without ever touching the scotch glass, Benny pulled his hand away from the bar. "Hey, I was only trying to offer my condolences you fuckin' asshole," he snipped, all the gayness back in his voice. Then he turned and swished off into the crowd as Michael Lawson moved in beside me.

"Two Bellinis," Lawson said to the bartender. And to me he said: "You ever think of taking a Dale Carnegie course?"

"I did. I failed."

Admiring how fast Benny thought on his feet, I took both tumblers of scotch from the bar and said to Michael Lawson, "Excuse me, I need to get this drink to a real man."

Knowing Michael Lawson was watching, I crossed the room and held out the scotch for Andy to take.

"What the hell's this?"

Maria looked at me as if I had just lost my mind. She knew Andy didn't drink.

"Just take it."

"You're becoming a real putz," Andy said, taking the glass.

"Gee, I must be in good form tonight. The queer just called me an asshole."

"Good call," Andy agreed.

"See any killer-eyes watching our Fargo girls?" I said, sliding my arm around Maria's waist.

Andy grunted.

"Give it up, partner," he said. "For over two months now you've been consumed with finding a killer that hasn't left a single clue. Let it rest. It's one thing to be crazy enough to risk your own ass. But now you've got this kid involved."

"I never expected her to be crazy enough to dress up like she wanted to be killed."

We both looked at Maria. She turned her head away, obliviously annoyed with our parental attitude.

"Maybe you'd like to meet the man himself," she said, staring across the room.

"What?"

"Over there," she nodded.

Fashionably late, Virginia was making her grand entrance. On her arm, instead of the Marc Jacobs shopping bag this time, she now toted a tall, lanky, sallow faced man, dressed in a black tuxedo jacket with purple lapels and sequined shoulders and blue jeans with

Dockers loafers. His invitation must have stated it was a no-tie, no-socks event.

I took him for twenty-nine, thirty at the most. His hair was moussed straight back, forcing a high forehead. His face wore the in-vogue perpetual five-o'clock shadow that matched half the young men in the room.

Virginia wore a black silk dress so tight around her midriff it gave her the rippled look of an overstuffed sausage.

The two double air-kissed their royal way through the drove of peons who came up to bask in their aura.

In the shadow of her partner and their number one client, Loretta Devon followed a few steps behind, wearing a black silk tuxedo jacket and pants that fit her very well.

"So that's the great Fargo," I said.

"Yeah," Maria chuckled.

"His whole name is Vinny Fargomatto," Andy said.

I smirked a how-come-you-know-this-kind-of-shit look at my partner.

"Get your stuffy head out of the *Financial Times* once in a while," Andy quipped.

This kid Fargo, who probably never had a real friend in his life, was strutting about like he was the most important person in the world.

As each young man and woman approached to bask in the aura of this designer of shrouds, my anger grew. What the hell was it with these kids? They cruised through life from one god to the next. Or was it one devil to the next?

Well, whichever, I figured, it was time to put on my salesman's smile again. *The devil you know is better than the devil you don't* know. So I took Maria by the arm and we too stepped into the aura.

"Mr. Fargo."

"Fargo. Just plain Fargo."

"Fargo." I smiled even wider, hearing the first truth of the night. "I had to come over and tell you how much I love how your design looks on my girlfriend."

I turned to Maria. "Maria? Didn't I say how beautiful you looked in this outfit? Didn't I?"

Maria smiled. "Oh, Jack just couldn't wait to see me in it."

"Yes, it does improve your waistline. But you must do something with your hair. Don't you think so, Ginny?" Fargo remarked.

Maria and I smiled, waiting on Ginny's response.

"Yes, you're like sooo right, Marie—" she began.

"Maria," I corrected the A-hole.

"Sorry. Maria...I must get you in touch with my hair stylist. She's like the very best. Hard to get an appointment with. But for me Mona will do anything."

"Oh yes, Maria. You must. I mean like I heard Ginny speak so glowingly of Mona when I dropped in at Kirk and Devon."

"So now you tell me," Maria baited me. "I can *like just die.*"

"What can I say?" I said, taking the bait. "I'm such a putz. Anyway, you look beautiful to me."

"Yeah sure. That's because you're imagining the thong I'm wearing. Forget about it. You ain't seeing any of it tonight."

Fargo stood smirking at the old fool and his bimbo.

"How about I buy a Fargo dress designed especially for you? How about that, Fargo?

"Will ya?" Maria sucked in her cheeks so her lips puckered. She leaned back on one stiletto heel, her arms crossed against her chest, squinting with an attitude. I gave her the Oscar for Best Performance in a Supporting Role.

"What do say, Fargo? Do me a solid. Get me in good with my girl again."

"Mister? Uh.. What did you say your name was?"

"Mr. Centaur," Virginia interjected.

"You can call me Centaur. Just, plain, Centaur."

"Centaur," Fargo grinned. "Like the mythical god. Half man and half..."

"Horse's ass." I smiled over to Maria.

"So whadaya think, Centaur?" Vinny from Brooklyn went on, "MY exclusive designs come cheap?"

"Tell him, Ginny, will you?" I grinned. "Tell your client here. When Centaur is after something, he's willing to pay the price."

Virginia took a deep breath, and as if for the first time seeing the man who stood before her, let it out, and said, "Mr. Centaur is Candice Nolen's uncle."

Fargo titled his head. "Whose uncle?"

I dropped my smile. This piece of gutter-shit who I didn't respect enough to send around the corner to pick up coffee couldn't recall the name of someone found dead in one of his *creations.*

"You must forgive Fargo for his insensitivity," Loretta broke in, stepping up now to join us. "He suffers from severe attacks of brain farts."

Virginia now grabbed Fargo's arm, saying "Dear Candice was the beautiful young woman who was taken from us by the horrible person out to destroy you."

Fargo's face remained blank.

"The Fashion Killer," Loretta cued him.

"Oh, oh, your niece? Dead?" Fargo remarked, still clueless. Then added, "Sorry, Centaur. But you gotta understand. I pay no attention to the newspapers. They're all just so against me."

"That's right," Virginia said. "They think my client is just a fad." I noticed Loretta bristle at the inference the word *my* carried.

"They don't respect my work," Fargo said, turning towards his publicist.

I stared at this smug idiot, thinking of how many times a week, in every cafe in town, I've heard that mantra of the non-talented: *they don't respect my work.*

"How much, Fargo? How much for one special design for Maria."

"Uh…five thousand dollars," Fargo took a shot.

"Sold!"

Fargo coughed. Sputtered. Tried to say something. Gagged. Turned pale over receiving so much *respect* for his work.

I was smiling now, thinking of how the tuxedo I had on cost more than the five grand I had just offered the putz.

Maria was bouncing. "Thank you. Thank you."

I caught Fargo, aka Vinny, checking out Maria's C cups, and didn't figure he was doing it to determine her dress size.

Virginia Kirk Lawson, the publicist exuberant, excused herself. She was off to spread the buzz.

Now I put on the schmuck, shit-eating-grin of an old man about to get the best lay of his life.

"Five thousand dollars is a great sum to pay to get what you want," Loretta Devon said.

"The end justifies the means, Ms. Devon," I replied.

"Justifies to whom, Mr. Centaur?"

"To the one seeking justice, Ms. Devon."

"I suppose you may be right, Mr. Centaur," Loretta said in a way that made me feel she was talking as much to herself as she was to me.

I GLANCED AT my watch. It was 1:12 AM. And I wasn't a bit closer to finding the killer than I had been at eight o'clock. Not a hint. Not a damn thing pointing me in any direction other than home.

"Let's call it a night," I finally said.

"So you're giving this Sherlock shit up?" Andy asked.

"Not a chance."

"I'll take her home," Andy said, turning to Maria.

"No. I will," I argued. "I'm not letting her out of my sight."

"Damn idiot," my partner muttered and headed for the door.

The event may have been a Young Metropolitans League benefit, but at the center of the ballroom, taking all the kudos, stood Bradford Lawson beside his third-wife, a 29-year-old former model who had been known by only one name, Brianna. Michael and Virginia stood a few well-measured feet away, catching the overflow.

Maria and I took our turn bidding the Lawson clan good night.

The last thing I heard as I escorted Maria from the ballroom was the sound of a very gay voice mocking, not-so-under-his-breath: "They should only make a law against Viagra."

SEVENTEEN

MARIA LIVED IN A THIRD floor walk-up on East Tenth Street off Broadway. A New York dream—a rent-controlled studio flat in a pre-war building. The checkerboard-size vestibule behind the steel entrance door from the street was a claustrophobic prelude to the rooms behind door number 3G. I entered a kitchen only a bit larger than the vestibule. Pressed against the wall, beneath an ancient double-hung window, stood a small white vinyl-topped kitchenette table with blue-enameled legs. Only two chairs: one on the right of the table, the other chair facing the window. A steam radiator occupied the place for a third chair. The window looked out onto a courtyard pocketed on four sides by the rear windows of a hundred similar apartments.

Through the kitchen there was another, even smaller room, call it an area, with a small couch and a television on a rolling stand and a steel dress rack, that did double duty as Maria's living room and clothing closet. The third room was Maria's bedroom. I remained in the kitchen.

Maria said I was crazy for insisting on spending the night, but I figured so far none of the Fashion Killer's victims had been murdered by daylight, so I was parking myself at that kitchen table until sunrise. And then I was taking the damn Fargo outfit with me when I left, and burning the piece of crap. The hell with returning it to Devon!

My tuxedo jacket still on, my bowtie undone, I sat in the chair facing the window, nursing a mug of tea that had gone cold hours ago. The rain had stopped around 3 AM. By five-thirty the sky had turned a pale yellow, making the puddles in the courtyard look like pools of piss.

Maria had been right about what she had said at the gala about my "homophobic shit" getting me into enough trouble. I rubbed my temples wondering: *maybe I'm too old to understand it? I'm for sure of a different generation.* I knew of only one queer growing up. Demetri's older brother. At least everyone thought the brother Costas was queer. No one was certain. The kid stayed to himself, or sometimes mysteriously took the subway to Greenwich Village. And if anyone was crazy enough to broach the subject around Demetri, or if even a whisper reached his ears that one of the guys had hinted Costas was queer, Demetri would be kicking ass for a week. Demetri was big, and pumped iron everyday. He was out to prove that there were no faggots in his family. And, as for lesbians, hell, back then, if the girls were going down on each other, the guys never knew a thing about it. Hell, back then the guys didn't even believe girls masturbated. But that was all long ago, in a different world, and now, alone in Maria's kitchen, my fight with Candice haunted me.

Jesus, her teens went by without a problem. Smoked pot a few times. *So what? As long as it was only a few times.* She had a good head on her shoulders. She knew what lines not to cross. Then she hits nineteen and comes out. Didn't want to hide anything from anyone. *Especially from her Uncle Jack.* But her relationships were quick, and always failed.

What's wrong with seeing a shrink? Maybe it will help you? What's the matter? You think if someone is gay they must be sick in the head?

Yeah, yeah I know, it's politically incorrect to think that just maybe having a same-sex relationship might be a sign of an emotional problem!

You're one to talk. Fifty-six years old and never married. Never even lived with anyone. To you Uncle Jack, a relationship is a long weekend away somewhere.

Maybe my emotional problem is I'm just looking for the right woman to love?

Your problem Uncle Jack is I don't think you're capable of loving any woman.

"Get the hell out of here," I finally said. "Go ahead, do whatever the hell you want."

She slammed the door.

And that was the last time I had any contact with Candice.

But damn it! What the hell did Candice know anyway? She didn't come home from Nam to a dead girlfriend. She didn't get a letter: a letter Betty didn't want to write to me, but had to. What was I going to think after a couple mail calls and Sharon's letters didn't come? The orange envelopes with the A's in my name drawn like little valentines. Oh Candice, I was capable of loving!

Sharon wrote me every day, sometimes twice a day. She was waiting for me to come home. She was safe back in the world. I was the one in the boonies. I was the one who had been dealt the shitty hand. What was Sharon doing anyway? Just going to NYU. Just standing on a goddamn subway platform waiting for a train. That's all Sharon Weiner was doing—this nineteen-year-old woman whom I couldn't possible know how to love—when a bunch of scumbags get into a gang fight and bullets start flying. Why the hell are bullets flying in a subway station in Brooklyn? There were enough bullets in the air where I was. Yeah, Sharon takes a stray one to the head, and me, I get nothing. It was me who was supposed to get it. What the hell was wrong with God anyway? The fucked-up bastard! It was supposed to be Jack Centaur who gets it in the head. Didn't the bastard know that!

So God, you put those snipers in the bushes. Well I'd show you. Wouldn't I? God, you fuckin' missed. Here I am! Come and get me you stupid bastard! No—no, instead I get the Medal of Honor! What for? I wasn't trying to save anyone. I was only looking for God. To settle the score and let the son-of-a-bitch get it right this time!

Ah, what's the use? I couldn't have told Candice all that. Couldn't have told her how I came home, walked into a precinct and was told by some bulbous nose detective, two-sheets-to-the-wind, to go fuck myself. 'If you fuckin' guys would get it right over there and end that shit war then,' the cop said, 'I'd have the fuckin' time to go searching for a gang fuck, instead of working the hippy fuckin' demonstrations.'

No, I never told my niece. And I made Betty swear to keep my secret. It was my loss, wasn't it, after all? And I'd deal with it my own way. I didn't need anyone's sympathy.

THE LIGHTS FROM the courtyard apartments came on almost in unison. People were about to step into their morning shower; have their morning coffee; get ready to leave for work; drop the kids off at school. Every one of them doing their normal routine.

I slammed the tea mug down against the table. Candice was right! Who the hell was I to judge anyone?

"You okay, Jack?"

Maria came into the kitchen, a brown plaid flannel robe covering her from neck to ankles. Her bare feet tucked into a beat-up pair of green terry-cloth slippers, her hair all askew. She was a welcomed sight.

"You look like you slept well," I said, standing up.

Maria took three steps over to the sink. She ran cold water from a noisy faucet. Dampened a dishtowel. "Come here," she said.

A wedge of sunlight sliced through the top of the window. Maria squinted. I moved to block the sun from her eyes.

"When'd the rain stop?"

"Around three," I said.

"Been up all night?"

I wanted to tell her that the last time I had slept through an entire night was during the drunken binge I'd taken after Candice's funeral. Instead, I said: "You've got an insomniac woman across the yard who works out naked on a treadmill?"

"You mean the natural blond?"

"I never got past the great headlights."

"I'll bet," Maria said, pulling my right hand over the sink. She began dabbing the tea that had splashed onto my French cuff with the dishtowel.

I was about to say, "Thank you," when my cell phone rang. Startled, I reached awkwardly with my left hand into the breast pocket of my jacket.

Maria let go of my arm. I switched the phone to my right hand. "Hello."

"Where are you?" Dent asked.

I told him.

"A patrol car will be outside in five minutes."

I didn't need to ask why—the rancid taste of murder had returned to my mouth.

EIGHTEEN

THE APARTMENT WAS MONEY. OLD money. Filled with antique furniture and fine paintings. Not that shit Lawson hung. If you didn't peek out the window and see the late model Mercedes lining York Avenue you'd think you were living in the 1940's.

The body lay posed on a Persian rug. The Fargo dress pushed up to expose the black fishnet stockings.

"Her name is Susan Newcastle," Dent said, making meticulous notes into that memo pad of his.

To me, she was P-Cap.

"Go ahead, Weinberg," Dent said. "Take your picture."

I turned to see who the detective was speaking to, and this time the camera flash blinded me.

"Thanks, Detective," I heard a voice reply, but couldn't see the face, and then whoever he was, was gone.

"Who the hell was that?" I asked, rubbing my knuckles into my eyelids.

"Weinberg. Shoots pictures for the *Journal.*"

I opened my eyes. "So you just let him come in and take pictures!" An array of blue and yellow flash spots floated over Dent's face. "What the hell for?"

"Guy's makin' a fuckin' fortune with that camera," Frank Bark, the burly detective who had escorted me up to the apartment grunted.

"Some paper is gonna take 'em," Dent shrugged. "Polite guy, though. Not pushy."

Dent clicked his ballpoint shut. Clipped it to the memo pad and said, "You look like shit."

"Awake all night in stiff-backed chair will do that to a guy."

"Tell me about it."

"Decor doesn't fit a young kid." I said, scanning the room. "This her place?"

"She inherited it a couple months ago from her grandmother's estate." Dent nodded for me to move over to an alcove where we could speak out of earshot of the teams working the room for evidence.

"You two were at the same party last night. What can you tell me?"

"Not much. Only saw her for a few minutes. She was in front of me in line to buy play money."

"She with anyone?"

"Some guy. Real putz. Part of the clique from Club Faux Pas. Gets plastered on Coors Light. Got the impression he was just her escort, not her boyfriend. Maybe hoping to get lucky. I saw him trying to feel her ass. She wouldn't let him."

"Ever hear of Newcastle and Bennett?"

"The publishing house. Landmark Building on Fifth Avenue."

"Great granddaughter of Dean Newcastle. The guy whose money built the building."

"The Fashion Killer just moved high up on the social register."

"You catch on quick," Dent said "It's one thing to knock off starving models and secretaries. That stays local. Knock off a rich brat. Tabloids got something they can sell nationally."

"So this one's making *Entertainment Tonight*."

"Just what I need. Mayor's been down our throats as it is. Now he's going to be under a national microscope."

"So what happens now? Someone else takes over the case?"

"Not a chance," Dent shook his head. "He'll send in overseers and they'll louse up everything wanting updates every twenty minutes. But you can be sure of one thing—"

"Yeah. You're the fall guy if the scumbag isn't caught."

"You named that tune right buddy," Dent smirked

"Hope you get more manpower. You'll need it just to keep track of all the ladies dressed in Fargos. There were a least five women wearing Fargo designs last night. Including my date."

"Great."

"So why do you think our killer picked out Newcastle?" I asked. Perspiration was forming on the back of my neck, thinking the body might have been Maria's had I not stayed with her.

"Maybe she was the most accessible," Dent said. "She lived alone, for one thing."

"What about the date."

"Doesn't appear he stayed the night." Dent said. "The bed's still made."

"Maybe he had a stand-up quickie and a 'see ya later hon.'"

"So you're saying Newcastle wasn't a lesbian?"

"I didn't get the impression she was." I said.

"Then we've got a change in MO?"

"We, Kemosabe?"

Dent looked at me as if I were nuts. "KemmoWha—"

"Forget it," I grunted. The joke was too old to explain.

Dent shook his head. "Let's follow the angles," he said, and continued brainstorming. "If we eliminate lesbians, we still have the Fargo dress?"

"And the Lawson connection," I reminded Dent.

"What's your take on that?"

"Don't know," I shrugged. "Michael and Virginia make a strange couple. The wife totally freaks out finding a dead body. She calls her husband's cell and Mikey practically beams himself up to the suite, he's there so fast. Yet, he's cool enough to spend five minutes waiting for his old man to not return his call before finally calling 9-1-1."

"Conditioned reaction." Dent said. "Call Daddy. He'll fix everything."

"That's pretty much what Virginia told me. But I'm not buying it. At least not until I find out where old and young Lawson were at the time my niece was being laid out for a front page spread."

"Enough people saw them at the party to give them an alibi," Dent said.

"Or at least saw them at times. The doesn't mean either of them stayed there all the time."

"Bradford Lawson's all over my bosses," Dent said. "I got my marching orders to step carefully around his people."

"Is that why you didn't have any undercover cops at the party last night?"

"We tried. But Lawson would have none of it. Says the murders are connected to his agency only because of his daughter-in-law's connection to Fargo. Says it's all about who ever Fargo screwed."

"Right," I shook my head. "How could anyone ever have a grudge against a double-crossing, welching, egotistical prick like Bradford Lawson?"

Bark called out from the living room.

"Be right there," Dent shouted back. And to me he warned, "Don't forget about not pushing the envelope too far."

Our partnership was laid out firm that morning. Dent wasn't about to allow a bunch of political schmucks screw up the investigation, and his career along with it.

I thought this alliance would be good up to a point. I'd use Dent for information. What wasn't good was I had partnered up with a man of principles. Dent wanted to bring the killer in alive if possible. Do it by the book. Miranda and all. And me? I looked over at P-Cap lying dead on her grandmother's antique rug, and wanted just one thing—a clean kill.

NINETEEN

THERE'S NO DRESS CODE IN the Starlight Diner. A man comes in with a two-day growth on his face, wearing a rumpled tuxedo and a tea-stained white shirt cuff; he gets a seat in a booth by the window next to a guy in a Brooks Brothers pinstripe.

I glanced at the menu and, without looking up, told the waitress, "Make it the number 2. It fits the way I feel."

The guy in the pinstripe got up from the booth, took one last quick sip of coffee, accidentally knocking his copy of *The New York Journal* he had left at the edge of the booth-bench onto the floor. The headline read: FASHION KILLER SOCIETY HIT.

Pinstripe glanced down at the paper, and up to the man in the next booth staring down at it, who looked as though he'd had a really rough night and said, "You can have the paper." Then he threw a buck tip down on the table and rushed off to the cashier without another word.

My city was ugly again. New Yorkers had made a miraculous comeback from bankruptcy and the garbage piled streets of the 70's. They beat the crack, crime and AIDS of the 80's. In the 90's they cleaned Times Square of porno shops and hookers, and transformed it into the Wonderful World of Disney.

Then with the new millennium came September 11th and the fear of terrorists pervaded the city. Now children were holding parent's hands tightly as they looked up at Times Square's kaleidoscope of digital marquees while walking passed teams from the NYPD Special

Units brandishing M16's like grunts from Nam. And over at Grand Central Station, National Guardsmen stood donned in camouflage fatigues and 9-millimeter pistols.

New Yorkers had learned to accept the fate of the world's other great cities. To tolerate the show of force on their streets. To accept, even to respect the cops, who stopped them before passing through the subway turnstiles, asking politely to inspect the backpack or the briefcase they innocently carry. Mothers didn't complain when baby strollers were searched. Skyscrapers evacuated of office workers, while dogs like the ones that sniffed out booby traps in Vietnam, sniffed suspicious boxes lying in stairwells. Only to discover the box was nothing more than someone's unfinished lunch.

Yes, I felt my city was ugly again. But I knew whoever was killing these young women was not a terrorist from outside. And that made for a different kind of ugly.

And now the whole ugly mess was staring up at me from the floor of the Starlite Diner. I reached down and scooped P-Cap up, wondering how the rag had hit the street so fast? The small type below the crime scene photograph read: *"I wouldn't be caught dead in one" is not what the celebutants draped in death-row fashions from bad-boy designer Fargo were saying when they challenged The Fashion Killer by dancing under the chandelier of the Pollock Ballroom at a Young Metropolitans Benefit last night…*

I turned the page and there spread across pages two and three, were all the front-page photographs of the four other victims. First to last. And there again, I saw that shot of Candice once more.

My eggs turned cold on the plate. The tea tasted like battery acid. Then it hit me as fast and as hard as the F-Train. The angle I had missed. *Damn it! The pictures! The Fashion Killer has some ghoulish reason for seeing these pictures make the front page. Why else pose the bodies?*

Did Fargo think it was the only way he could get his designs into print? Was he that bad of a bad-boy? Or was Virginia Kirk-Lawson the publicist from hell? Was her drive to outdo the other trust-fund publicists of the city so warped she'd kill to win?

And the *Journal's* editors?—they were just as much a part of the crime. They'd milk that picture of P-Cap in four issues a day, every day for weeks. Just as they had run the others. Just as they had run my niece's.

I noticed now for the first time the small photo credit type in the white space border of every picture, the name of Irwin Weinberg.

Why was his picture always the "Exclusive First Photograph"?

'Someone's gonna take it,' Dent had said.

'Guy's makin' a fortune with that camera,' Bark had said.

'Nice guy though,' Dent had so casually commented.

"Yeah, so what's Weinberg's angle in all this?" I asked myself.

It was time to see the face behind the flash.

TWENTY

IT TOOK WHAT WAS LEFT of the morning to meander through the phone maze of *The New York Journal,* hanging up on a dozen voice-mail recordings, until I finally got to some guy in the city department who said Irwin Weinberg was not an employee, but a freelance photographer.

I asked the guy if he had a phone number Weinberg could be reached at and the guy laughed. "You gotta be kiddin' me. Everything's done by e-mail around here." And then he gave me Weinberg's e-mail. It was as simple as that.

I had lied to Michael Lawson for effect. I did "do" e-mail. I shot one off to Weinberg. Gave him my name, and who Candice Nolen was to me. Put my cell number into the e-mail. It rang within minutes.

"Jack Centaur." The voice was polite. "Irwin Weinberg. How can I be of help?"

"I must have caught you sitting in front of your computer."

"Blackberry."

"Of course," I said. "Look, I'd like to meet with you."

"I'm puzzled? Why were you at the crime scene this morning?"

"How'd you know who I was?"

"I remembered seeing you…" Weinberg's voice trailed off.

"Standing over my niece when you shot her picture."

"Yes," Weinberg paused, and then asked again, "So why were you standing over Newcastle's body this morning?"

"That's what I need to see you about."

"I don't understand."

"Did you mean it when you asked how you could be of help? Or were you just being polite? Dent says you're a real polite guy."

"I just take pictures. That's all. But if you think I can be of help, then of course I'll meet with you."

"How about I buy you dinner."

"Tonight?"

"Elaine's. Nine o'clock"

"Elaine's? Nice. Can you get a reservation?"

"See you at nine."

"Okay...sure," Weinberg said, his voice still obliging. "I'll catch you at nine."

TWENTY-ONE

HAD MADE A DATE for tonight with the crime photographer extraordinaire, and now I was going to use the afternoon to shake things up down on the Lower Eastside.

When I arrived at the Eldridge Street address Dent had given me, there weren't any corporate signs on the six-story apartment building. I searched the sun-faded green plastic nameplates next to the bank of buzzers to find the name NWF. The letters stood for Nelka, Wayne and Fargo. The nameplate hadn't changed, even though it was nine months since the F had left the building. And just a week before the first murder!

I rang the buzzer three times before someone finally screamed down from a top floor window, "What the fuck you want?"

I arched my neck back to see that the voice was coming from a ball of hair with a long, sliver protruding from the middle that I took to be a nose. "To kick Fargo's ass," I shouted up. The Hair-Head disappeared. The front door buzzed open.

Shit! No elevator. I climbed the twelve flights of steps to the sixth floor swearing all the way I would fill that Lipitor prescription I'd fought with my doctor about. I took a couple of deep breaths to lower my pulse rate before knocking on the door of 6-B.

When the door swung open, I had expected to see the hairball, not a six foot, bare-breasted, swim-thong clad blond goddess. Once I focused beyond her ring-pierced torpedoes, I spotted the hairball in the background. Except for his hairy head, the rest of his body was waxed from the neck to toe. All he had on was a white Speedo, with a bulge big enough to service whatever his six-foot partner needed.

"Enter." The Goddess's voice was as deep as a base drum.

I nodded, "Surf up?"

Brunhilda sneered: "Ve're working on da soommer line," and swung her torpedoes around. I feigned back, just inches out of striking range of the brass rings and followed her into the studio.

It looked as though someone had resurrected Warhol's Factory. The entire place was painted Day-Glo red. The heat was stifling. Metal steam radiators dating back to sometime before World War Two whistled up hot vapors that fogged, worn, thick-glazed double-hung windows. Hanging from the ceiling, a steel-pipe clothing rack serpentined the room.

"Great stingers," I said, referring to the two scorpions the blond had tattooed on the cheeks of her ass: the left scorpion, yellow; the right one, blue.

"Hey, Nelka we got some kind of fuckin' comedian here," Hair-Head said, sounding like a Jewish cabbie from Brooklyn. "So tell me? What happened? You woke up this morning hung over and remembered you ordered a five-grand piece of drek from a knock-off artist and now you come here to kick his ass. Forgetaboutit! We threw the scumbag motherfucker out of here months ago. You want him? Look for that fat twat publicist of his. And while you're at it, kick Vinny in those big balls of his a couple of times for us."

"News travels fast," I said, wondering how Hair-Head knew about my deal with Fargo. "So you're pissed off I commissioned your EX?"

"I'm pissed off that everything he sells we fuckin' designed first. Come here. You know what this is?" Hair-Head motioned me over to a large table and pushed a black leather portfolio toward me. "This is our look-book."

I turned the portfolio around and leafed through the clear vinyl pages. The drawings were similar to the designs the murder victims were found wearing.

"So tell me," I said, closing the look-book. "You'd rather see people dead in these than let your ex-partner make it big with them."

The partners stared at each like deer caught in car headlights.

"Whadaya fuckin' nuts or somethin'? You think we killed those no-talent models."

"One of those no-talent models was my niece, scumbag."

Hair-Head raised open palms in front on himself. "Look man, no offense. I wasn't thinking straight. You got me goin' here. I know…I know who you are. But, you gotta know we ain't no sickos."

I undid my tie. Removed my jacket. I rolled up my shirtsleeves. First the left, then the right.

Hair-Head took a step backwards. His partner took a step forward.

If I was going to have to fight anyone it looked like it would be Brunhilda. Figuring I knew her favorite position, I was pretty sure I was not going to come out on top.

"Lighten up," I said. "In case you haven't noticed, I didn't exactly come dressed for the beach."

I took a handkerchief from my pants pocket. Wiped my forehead, saying, "Whoever's committing these murders has definitely increased sales for Fargo."

"Yeah, so like what does that do for us?"

"Maybe the Fashion Killer's plan backfired," I said. "Maybe the Fashion Killer figured it would work like when the Son of Sam shot only girls who had long black hair. Remember how all over the city young girls cut their hair short and dyed it blond.

"Maybe the Fashion Killer figured if bodies started showing up dressed in Fargo designs no woman right in her mind would want to be found dead in anything he created."

"Whoze dis Son of Sam?"

"You know you're really off your rocker," Hair-Head laughed. "I was like three years old when Son of Sam was doin' his thing."

"You get what I mean," I said, feeling like a dinosaur.

"And you think we're that crazy. We'd actually go out killing people to get back at Vinny."

"It's not like you guys haven't gotten violent before."

"Come on, man. That was our thing. Got us press. Most of that shit was for show. Anyways," Hair-Head said, shrugging, "why should we? We got our own line coming out next summer. Yeah, that's right. And we're even talkin' with a big house about maybe having our own label in the fall. Fuckin' Vinny's gonna fade away once this killer's caught, and we'll still be in business."

"Maybe Fargo who is the one doing diz killing," Nelka said, folding her arms across her torpedoes.

"Could be," her partner chimed in. "Like you already said, he's the one getting the fame and glory. Not to mention, five grand from an old fart out to impress his little girl toy."

I gave Hair-Head a smirk that said, *you can't be that stupid.*

"Hey," Hair-Head was holding up his palms again. "I'm just quoting this morning's Page Six. Right here." He handed me *The New York Post.* "Read for yourself."

I leafed through the rag. Page Six hadn't been printed on a page six in years. I finally found it on page 15.

...Jack Centaur (Uncle of Fashion Killer Victim Candice Nolen) partied last night with his 25-year-old secretary at the Young Metropolitans League Benefit. The gathering at the Pollock Room was dazzled by Mr. Centaur's date's "borrowed" dress. A Design by Fargo! Hasn't Mr. Centaur seen enough of the ghoulish dressmakers' work? Seems not. Page Six has been told by a source very, VERY close to Fargo that Uncle Big Daddy has consigned a $5,000 Fargo exclusive for his "secretary." OhMYGOD! She must do some great spreadsheet!...

Perfect! I hoped the rest of my plan worked out as well. If I only knew exactly what that plan was.

I handed the *Post* back to Hair-Head.

"So what's the reason you really came here?" Hair-Head tossed the newspaper onto the table.

"I told you. To kick Fargo's ass."

"Do you see FARGO anywhere around here."

"Actually..." I nodded.

On the far wall hung a life-size four-color poster of the three partners. All had on badass stares under a banner heading: NWF.

"To remember vhat a big mistake ve made."

"Why the bull's-eye?" I said, referring to three red rings drawn over their ex-partner's face.

"Because our target is to outsell him. Not to kill him. Or anyone else!"

"I want you two to make up a half-dozen designs for my girlfriend. I'll pay you six thousand apiece."

"Vhat about the von you ordered from Fargo?"

"I'm canceling it."

"He won't like that."

"That's not your problem."

I reached over to the table, slipped my hand inside my jacket and when it came out again I unfolded a check made payable to Cash and laid it flat on the table between Wayne and Nelka.

Brunhilda stared at the number: $36,000. Her brass rings rose up an inch.

I wasn't about to look over at what might have been rising in Hair-Head's Speedo.

TWENTY-TWO

A LONG WAY UPTOWN FROM the hustle of the Westside theater district and midtown publishing houses, Elaine draws celebrities to her dark, no-tech saloon like bats to a cave.

I wasn't a celebrity. But I'd been dining there for enough years that Elaine called me by my first name and gave me a regular table just past the wall of fame, beneath the alabaster bust of George Plimpton.

I had been in the same room with Weinberg twice before, yet, if my life depended on picking the man out of a lineup, I'd be dead. I had envisioned maybe a shoddily dressed old man lugging a big black box camera with a huge dish flash attachment hooked on top. Or, more likely, a high-tech, twenty-something digital whiz kid, with unkempt head hair and a three-day beard, wearing washed-out jeans and a T-Shirt.

I was pleased when the person who arrived promptly at nine o'clock was a well-groomed middle-aged man, dressed in what had to be at least a two-thousand-dollar rust-colored Armani sportcoat and a five-hundred-dollar black cashmere knit pullover shirt. The jacket and the pullover coordinated well with mid-gray wool slacks I'd bet were also Armani. The shoes were ostrich Italian loafers. I wouldn't have been surprised if Weinberg had purchased the entire ensemble in Milan. What I would never have imagined was Weinberg's odd complexion.

Not as ghostly white as the Plimpton bust, but neither the natural flesh tone of a Caucasian who manages to get out in the daylight every once in a while, either. Something else I didn't envision was Weinberg's clean-shaven head. Yet what hair the photographer lacked on his head he made up for with thick brown eyebrows and an even thicker, abbreviated Fu Manchu mustache. I sensed the stache might have, when Weinberg was young, gone down the full length of his strong, square chin. I had shaven my Fu Manchu off in 1975, for my first job interview with Stahl and White, Certified Public Accountants. I thought of growing it back again after quitting the CPA firm to join its floundering client, Smoothe Press, as Chief Financial Officer, and pulling it out of certain bankruptcy, but then I thought: What the hell for?

I had arrived at eight forty-five and already had my double Chivas in hand when Frank the waiter came up to the table and asked Weinberg, "Can I bring you anything from the bar?"

Weinberg said, "Islay, 12-year-old, straight up."

"Irwin," I said. "You don't exactly fit my image of a guy who shoots pictures of corpses."

"I had considered fashion photography," Weinberg smiled. "But I was over fifty, and not into kissing a twenty-something art director's ass at every publishing house to get a shoot. And I'm not the paparazzi type. There's not enough money in the world that'll get me into baggy Wal-Mart short pants, door-stepping to take a "candid" shot of some celebrity putz just out of rehab." Weinberg made air quotes when he said "candid."

Frank placed Weinberg's drink down on the table, and I questioned, "Over fifty?"

Weinberg took a slow sip of Islay, cocked his head with approval to Frank and said to me, "Midlife career move."

"Needed to reinvent yourself after the gas to start the old machine ran dry," I said. "A lot of that going around these days."

"You got it!"

"What was your first career?"

"Silicon Valley entrepreneur."

I swirled the ice in my empty drink glass.

"No shortage of bucks in that neck of the woods."

"I did well. Very well. But, I got tired of it. The pressure to always be 'the biggest.'" Air quotes again.

"Some people never come to that realization. They just drop dead at their desk."

"It took a real burnout to bring it home to me." Weinberg finished off his Islay and signaled Frank for another. I signaled for another double-Chivas.

"Midlife crisis? Call it what you want," Weinberg said. "But after busting my ass through Harvard Business School, then securing a job in a consulting firm—you know what the hell that is like?"

"About the same as working for a CPA firm?"

"You're a CPA?" Weinberg's raised his bushy eyebrows. "Maybe we can talk about a tax situation I have."

"Forget about it. My realization came about twenty years sooner than yours. I'm a partner in a printing factory now. I don't do outside tax work."

"Hmm. Your suit, Savile Row?" Weinberg motioned with hands. "A regular table at Elaine's? Didn't know there was so much money in printing."

"I've been known to dabble a bit here and there in other investment opportunities."

Weinberg arched an eyebrow.

Frank brought over our drinks and a couple of menus.

"Elaine's got the best veal chop in town," I said, cutting off Weinberg's Dunn and Bradstreet inquiry.

"Enjoy. I'm a vegan," Weinberg smiled. In the subdued lighting his teeth gleamed a very expensive bonded white.

"Frank, got anything for my vegan friend?"

"More Islay?" Frank said, flatly.

"A large plain green salad will be fine," Weinberg gleamed. "And if you have them? Lots of heirloom tomatoes."

"We got cherry tomatoes. That okay?"

"That'll work."

"So what happened?" I asked. "You took the proverbial leap from consulting to start-up."

"Exactly. Found some venture capital funds. Went into manufacturing microchips. Didn't exactly corner the market, but we did make a nice niche for ourselves producing chips for laser printers. It was 24/7, with my venture capitalist partners all over me to turn the start-up into a "Fortune 1,000 company" at least.

"I was traveling all over the world. Jet lag was my normal state of being. If I ever got in more than three hours sleep in one night, I'd wake up freaking out that I'd wasted valuable time. I'm telling you it was crazy. But when you're living it, you don't see it. The anxiety attacks. The paranoia. You tell yourself it's just the effects of the jet lag. Jack, we can really bullshit ourselves good when we set high goals."

I muttered something about goals being heroine to the business mind.

Frank brought over my twenty-six ounce veal chop. And Weinberg's pile of grass.

"So when did this realization come?"

"Within ten years we were doing $800 million dollars in sales. I had eighteen hundred employees—six vice presidents, and a Board of Directors from hell. We all had options. Took the business public. Everyone was wired to push the stock shares up. Shit, I'd bet you, Jack, the Blackberry kills more people today then car accidents. You're never out of the reach of someone who wants a piece of you, and wants it immediately.

"And I was as wired-up as anyone. I pushed my people to their limits—sometimes beyond. One of my VP's, a guy with me right from the start-up, drove his Lamborghini off a lookout point up in Mendocino.

"Witnesses said he got out of the Lamborghini, looked over the guard railing, and then casually strolled back to the car. Got in. And floored it. Sailed the Lamborghini two hundred feet down to the rocky beach.

"That was it for me. I worked out a deal with my partners. Cash. Options. Non-compete. Got out of the business. This time I traveled for pleasure only. Took a camera, and headed off to parts unknown.

Never married. So I had no attachments. I just took off for five years of blowing in the breeze."

Weinberg paused. "Your veal is getting cold. Mangia. I've been talking your head off."

"Not at all," I said. "You're an interesting guy, Irwin. Can't say that I haven't felt the same way at times. You know, you start out wanting to kick the world's ass and when you finally do, it doesn't really matter that much to you anymore. That's when all of a sudden it seems like the world's kicking *your* ass."

Weinberg looked down at the mass of cherry tomatoes in the middle of his salad. Stuck his fork into one, looked across to me as if we'd been old friends separated for years, and asked, "How you holding up?"

"Not great," I admitted for the first time to anyone, including myself.

"Time. At our age Jack, we both know, in time, the pain passes. The memory dulls a little and we learn to move on."

I pushed the untouched veal chop aside.

"Thanks for your concern. I mean it. Really. Only I didn't ask you here to help me wallow in self-pity. I want you to help me find the bastard."

"What can I do? I just take the pictures. Sell them to the *Journal*. Make my money. And—"

"And wait until The Fashion Killer strikes again."

"Jack, it's a business. I'm just doing my thing."

"Ever think maybe seeing your pictures on the front page is what's driving this fiend?"

"No. But, if it is, that's not my fault. I wasn't there directing the first layout."

"Layout!"

"Murder. Sorry. Just, I mean—"

"You mean that it becomes abstract to you after a while. Just a body on the floor," I said. I understood he meant no harm. I knew his headset. I had felt the same way in Vietnam. After a while the dead become just that: bodies. Not someone who once lived.

"All I did was get there in time to take the first picture. That's how you make the big bucks in this business. Be at the scene first. Better still, get the 'exclusive shot.'"

"Yeah, what about that?" I asked. "How come you're always the first photographer at the crime scene."

"You ever hear of a crime photographer called Weegee?'

"Back in the 40's. Worked for the Daily News. Took shots of murders, accidents, Mob rubouts. Real noir stuff."

"That's right. Except he didn't actually work for the Daily News. Arthur Felig, that's his real name. Used the name Weegee because he thought it sounded mysterious. You know, like the Ouija board. Go figure. Anyway, he was a freelancer. Top in the business. Do you know his work is considered art today?"

"Yes. I caught an exhibit of his work a couple of years ago," I said, remembering a show at the Whitney Museum.

"See. That's what I'm talking about. I want my pictures to be considered in his league. While I was doing all that traveling, taking pictures of everything, the creative juices started to flow again. It was a rejuvenation. You know that B-school sticks with you. I started saying to myself, "Okay now how can I make some money out of taking pictures?"

I grinned.

"Yeah, I know what you're grinning about," Weinberg smirked. "What do I need the money for? Well if you believe goals are the heroine, then money is the syringe. So I put the old B-school training to a new field. Like I said, fashion photography is for the young. Paparazzi? No way. So what was left? National Geographic? Maybe. But in my B-plan research I hit on Weegee. The guy was making a fortune selling his shots to the highest bidder. How did he get those great shots? How did he get to the scene before anyone else with a camera? Networking! He had paid people on the inside. He'd go so far as to put cops in the picture. They were all his friends. A rubout. An accident. Whatever. Weegee showed up first. The rest of the media had to settle for hind tit."

"You've got a contact in the police department who is on the take?"

Weinberg shrugged. "Let's just say I have a good network."

I studied the man sitting across the table from me. I envied his passion because I had none anymore. Hadn't in years.

"Anything wrong?" Frank asked, noticing we hadn't touched our entrées.

"No Frank, food's fine. We're just not as hungry as we thought."

Frank lifted our full plates from the table. When he left, I said to Weinberg, "I want you to stop selling your photos. Take them off the market."

Irwin Weinberg pulled his square chin into his neck. "This is how I can help you?"

Frank returned, setting two brandy snifters down. "With Elaine's compliments," he said, and left.

"Are you nuts?" Weinberg continued. "You want me to put myself out of business. I've got a book deal going. Show all my work, not just the Fashion Killer pieces. You know I was doing very well before all these murders."

"Actually, I didn't know. But that works even better for you."

"For me? How do figure I'll benefit from this scheme of yours?"

"You'll get tons of publicity. It will further separate you from the rest of the pack. Come on, does anyone really look at your little name in the white space. You may be known to the rest of the wolves in the business, but Joe Six-Pack, he just sees the picture, not the photo credit."

"So how does that change when there's not even a picture for Joe Six-Pack to see?"

"Come on, Harvard B-School man. What a marketing gimmick. You remove the photos because you somehow feel responsible for perpetuating the murders. Your conscience is bothering you for helping to glorify the Fashion Killer. Shit, Oprah herself will be at your door. And just think about how the sale of your book will do then. Of course, you can make another grandstand play by promising that you will not release a book until the killer is caught."

Weinberg pulled the brandy snifter close, inhaled the sweet fragrance the monastery monks had instilled in it. He placed the thin rim of the snifter to his lips. Tilted his head back. His dark eyes swayed left, over my shoulder, to the framed book jacket covers hanging along the Wall of Fame. Took a sip. Sat the snifter down. His index finger slowly traced a water ring on the wooden table.

I sat silent. Andy had taught me that little trick only the great salesmen know. Once you've made your pitch: shut up.

"How does this get you any closer to finding the Fashion Killer?" Weinberg asked.

"Serial Killers want to be caught. Berkowitz…Kaczynski…all communicated with someone and were exposed. Isn't it strange that the Fashion Killer has been quiet? Not a letter to the press. Nothing."

"I still don't get it."

"Simple. The pictures. You know the saying. The medium is the message. Your pictures are the message, whatever that message might be. And no pictures—no message."

Weinberg looked again at the Wall of Fame and softly considered that. "Pictures are removed from sight, Fashion Killer gets frustrated, reaches out to someone in the media. Writes a letter."

"Yes."

"And gives up a clue that gets him caught."

"Yes."

Weinberg shrugged. "So I just call the *Journal*, saying I'm pulling my photographs. I can do that. I own the copyright. Can't be published anywhere without my permission."

"I don't want you to call the *Journal*. I want you to call Bradford Lawson."

"Lawson?"

"You tell him what you want to do. That you want to make the announcement on his cable show."

"Lawson's ego will lap it up," Weinberg laughed. "The Bradford one-ups city's officials again."

"And it'll get Irwin Weinberg, Crime Photographer, right out there in front of Joe Six-Pack."

"Jack there's one big flaw in your plan. If there is another murder—and I hope to God there isn't—and I don't do the shoot, there's always someone else waiting in the wings who will."

"There won't be another murder. I promise you that."

"And once The Fashion Killer is locked up my book will make me another fortune. That's what you think?"

"Even more if The Fashion Killer is found dead."

"Dead!"

"And Irwin Weinberg shoots"—it was my moment to air-quote—"'the exclusive first picture.'"

TWENTY-THREE

No, I couldn't ever have imagined Weinberg door-stepping with the paparazzi. Hanging over fences, climbing every tree limb outside the Newcastle family's Long Island estate waiting for that candid shot that will earn the lucky shooter a six-figured price. Whatever hope this wolf pack had of photographing a grieving Newcastle was lost when a family spokeswoman, dressed in a neat business suit, two private security men at her side, came out to stand in front of the estate's iron gates.

Cameras flashing. Video cams humming. Microphones jutting at her face. She never flinched, imparting the words of Susan Newcastle's parents. "Ronald and Emily Newcastle's hearts and prayers go out to the family and friends of all the other victims who have suffered the loss of a loved one to this most hideous and sadistic fiend. The Newcastle family will cooperate in every way possible with the authorities in the hope of apprehending The Fashion Killer. Now, at this time, the Newcastle Family asks they be given the privacy to mourn the loss of their beloved Susan with dignity."

An hour later Bradford Lawson used no spokesperson to convey his message. He had called a handpicked group from the press and television into his boardroom.

Standing beneath oil portraits of his father and his grandfather, Bradford Lawson made his grandstand play to upstage the Newcastle Family. "Tonight," he announced, "on a special LIVE broadcast of my Cable-1 television show, Lawson Speaks, I will have a *very* special guest. A guest who is close to the situation. A guest who has come to me, BRADFORD LAWSON, with a desire to make a moral, and a *HUGE* financial, sacrifice to aid in the capture of The Fashion Killer."

The boardroom broke into a frenzy. Reporters shouted questions at Lawson: "Who's so close to the situation? What will be sacrificed?"

Lawson assured everyone he, and only HE, knew the name of the guest and what was to be sacrificed. "Not even my closest confidantes will know the person's identity until LAWSON SPEAKS airs LIVE! Tonight."

Then, Lawson stared sternly into the television camera and said, "Everyone must tune in tonight for this will be a monumental event."

I clicked off my television.

Dent rose from my couch. "Where's Weinberg now?" he asked.

"I guess he's fine-tuning his B-plan."

"Wish *you* would have fined-tuned *your* plan with me first."

"Let's just hope The Fashion Killer has an ego as big as Lawson's."

TWENTY-FOUR

THE PULSE OF NEW YORK City can be found on the bent elbows of the patrons in Pete's Tavern. At 7:30 p.m. I parked myself on the last empty stool at the far end of the bar, my back to the old wooden cashier's cage that has sat for a hundred-and-fifty years in the same place before the entrance to the main dining room. A young woman sat in the cage sorting mint-green restaurant checks.

I got a whatyahave nod from the bartender—a white-haired gent wearing a short-sleeved, navy blue golf shirt, embroidered on the heart-side with *Pete's Tavern Since 1864.*

I asked for a pint of Pete's Ale.

The bartender placed a cocktail napkin and brown plastic bar-dish of popcorn in front of me. He moved a few feet down the bar, pulled a draft of ale, expertly letting the foam cascade, returned, placed the pint down on the cocktail napkin and turned, leaving me to my beer, and he grunted another whatyahave to some new patron.

The muted light emanating up through the translucent shades of the brass lamps along the bar hit the brown-painted tin ceiling, reflecting a pallid hue onto the faces below. By 7:45 PM the place was packed, the air thick with a cacophony of barroom bullshit.

At 8 PM I looked above the sea of heads to watch the bullshit that was now about to enter the room from the only concession the management of Pete's had made to the 21st century: A flat-screen television.

The opening camera shot moves in a slow pan, crossing a plush studio set. A mahogany coffee table. A long, deep-tufted leather couch. On stage right, what Lawson must think his best side, sits an equally deep-tufted high-back executive chair. The camera pans past the furniture to the mahogany paneled wall with large gold lettering: LAWSON SPEAKS. The letters so highly polished they reflect a mirrored glimpse of the hand-held television camera, and the union-man holding it. The cameraman moves and the well-rehearsed glimpse disappears as the two words part into a door in the mahogany wall, and Bradford Lawson makes his grand entrance.

His lips pressed into a tight smile, he nods, acknowledging those cheering in the studio, as he walks to center-stage. He holds a hand up. The cheers dissipate. LAWSON SPEAKS:

"A great tragedy has befallen this great city of ours. Five young women have been murdered. Cruelly murdered. Taken in the prime of their lives by a sadistic maniac who gets off on posing the bodies as if in a fashion magazine.

"As many of you know, one of my companies—one of my many companies—happens to be Lawson Worldwide Modeling. And, of course, in our employ are some of the finest, most glamorous models in the business. So you can only imagine how deeply these deaths have touched us.

"I stated in a press briefing earlier today at my offices at Lawson World Tower, we at Lawson Worldwide are fully cooperating with NYPD, the GREATEST law enforcement department on the face of the planet, in their effort to find this monster.

"It is my belief that this so-called Fashion Killer is feeding off the media attention. And that whoever the fiend is, they will continue to kill for the pure joy of seeing their awful deeds spread across the front pages of our newspapers. It is with this in mind that I have made a special appeal to our guest tonight. An appeal I must say was immediately agreed to by my special guest. A man of great integrity. Without further ado I'd like to introduce my very, very special guest. A person I'm proud to call my new friend. Mr. Irwin Weinberg."

Through the same door Lawson had entered slowly enters a very subdued Irwin Weinberg. The crowd claps a tentative applause, wondering who the hell is this bald, anemic man coming around the couch to shake the host's outstretched hand.

Weinberg plays his part well. He checks his ego at the door. He stands humbly beside Lawson. He's wearing the photographer's uniform: black slacks, black knit shirt and black sports jacket. He's at least five inches shorter than Bradford Lawson. Beneath the harsh, bright studio lights, Lawson's glistening hair-sprayed comb-over is pasted so far down his forehead it almost touches his thin blond eyebrows, while Weinberg's bald head looks as smooth as a baby's bottom. Lawson's clean-shaven face is in stark contrast to Weinberg's dark moustache and thick, Groucho Marx eyebrows. Weinberg and Lawson are the perfect odd couple, bonded by the glue of their egos.

Lawson looks into the camera. "You may not recognize his name," he says. "But you have seen it. Irwin Weinberg is the best crime photographer in the business. His photographs sell upward to—" Now Lawson is punctuating the air with his finger, emphasizing each word. "—one…hundred…thousand…dollars."

Lawson, silent, waits for the audience to react. There's murmuring in the studio. And murmuring in Pete's Tavern. With the timing of a circus ringmaster LAWSON SPEAKS:

"It is Weinberg's name you see in the copyright print next to the photographs of The Fashion Killer's victims."

The studio audience jeers.

"A-hole," I hear the young woman in the cage mutter.

Lawson holds up his hands. Puckers his thick lips in a way that says "now….now." The audience noise fades. LAWSON SPEAKS:

"My friend, Irwin, is a very nice man, working in an extremely competitive industry. One that puts him face-to-face with horrific scenes. He sees things that would turn most of our stomachs. But it's a job! And when done well, as Irwin's work is, the job of crime photographer serves history. The crime photographer records for posterity the harsh reality of his times. And, rightfully so, he gets paid well for his efforts. Yet, tonight Mr. Weinberg has a surprising—a startling!—announcement." Now it is Lawson who plays the humble card. Bowing, he steps aside, saying, "Please, Irwin, the stage is yours."

Weinberg clears his throat.

"I have been asked," Weinberg, clears his throat a second time. Begins again. "I have been asked by Mr. Lawson, and I have agreed, to pull all my photographs of the victims from print until the Fashion Killer is apprehended."

Loud cheering in the studio. The camera pans the audience rising in ovation. The camera pans back to a very smiling Bradford Lawson now patting Weinberg's back. Weinberg is humble, bowing his shaven head to the camera.

"Quiet. Please. Quiet." Lawson's open palms held up, instructs the audience. "My friend has more to say."

Weinberg raises his head and stares into the camera. "I appeal to all those who work in my field to place a moratorium on publicizing this monster." Weinberg's voice rises. "We need to stop feeding The Fashion Killer's psychotic mind. For the first time let us stop selling our souls for the exploitation of others."

Weinberg's words are broken by another burst of cheers.

Now Weinberg holds up open palms. The cheers soften, anticipating more sacrifice.

Weinberg does not disappoint. "I will," he promises, "donate all the money I have earned up to this point from the sale of my photographs of the victims to a special Victims' Relief Fund being set up by Mr. Bradford Lawson."

Lawson steps forward, positioned a few power-steps in front of his guest, nods that bouncing all-knowing nod of his and says, "In addition to the Victims' Relief Fund, tomorrow morning I will place $500 thousand into a special fund as a reward for anyone who can offer firm assistance that culminates in the capture of The Fashion Killer."

Whispering is heard from the studio audience. A wave of whispering runs thorough Pete's Tavern.

The Finale: The camera follows Lawson and Weinberg through the doors then turns, panning the cheering audience. Women are drying tears. Men are clapping hard, giving thumbs up. And inside Pete's Tavern the pulse of the city is beating strong.

• • •

I STEPPED FROM the darkness of the bar onto Irving Place, imagining how many ways I could shove Lawson's money up his ass.

There was still one question for Lawson to answer. *Where the hell was he when Candice lay dead on a bathroom floor?* Virginia said the Lawson kid tried for five minutes to get his father before giving up. She never said when her father-in-law finally did arrive at the scene. Or, for that matter, if the blow-hard had shown up at all.

It was now my turn to make Bradford Lawson speak.

TWENTY-FIVE

THE *DAILY NEWS* HEADLINE READ: LAWSON TO FASHION KILLER: I WANT YOU! The *Post's* had: FIVE...HUNDRED... THOUSAND...DOLLARS!!! And *The New York Journal's* had a full-page headshot, mid-word, mouth frozen wide open, headline shouting: LAWSON—BUCKS UP!

Which sounded a lot closer to what Dent was thinking when he called me.

"Thanks a lot! Every precinct phone in the city is ringing off the hook with morons hoping to cash in on the reward. The department's is going to be up to its ass in paperwork. I don't like this. Don't like it at all. Boss chewed my butt out this morning. And he got his butt chewed directly by the commissioner. And you can guess who's been chewing out the commissioner's butt. The mayor is not happy, my friend. Not happy at all!"

I knew if it were Lawson's money that caught The Fashion Killer, the newspapers would have a field day ripping apart the mayor's office. And it sure wouldn't be the first time that Lawson had trumped the mayor's office with an end-run around red tape.

I knew too, the city bosses wouldn't hesitate to make Dent the fall guy.

I had been holding the cell phone away from my head to take some of the bite from Dent's shouting. I pulled it closer now. "Take it easy," I said. "I'll get my shot at Lawson tonight. He's the guest speaker at my club."

"What?"

"It was set up months ago."

"There will be the board's usual Guest of Honor kiss-ass cocktail mingle before Lawson bullshits to regular membership about his family's contribution to the city's landscape."

"You're crazy if you think you can get anything out of that slick slime."

"I'm going to get something from him by the time the night is over."

"Yeah, good luck," Dent grunted.

"Oh, one more thing," I chided.

"What's that?" Dent snapped.

"It took until now to first figure out I'm crazy," I said, ending the call.

MAUREEN, THE VERY healthy waitress at the Broadway Diner, who gave a show every time she leaned over, poured more hot water to my cup of Earl Grey. I gave her a good glancing. "Like the eggs?" She smiled, knowing the nice tip she'd just secured. "Great yokes," I smiled back.

The tea water was scalding. And so was Tommy Convoy's column.

NOBODY KICKS UP DOUGH UNTIL THE RICH KID DIES

Cummings. Huy. Montrel. Nolen. All good, solid, straphanger names. Names the average working New Yorker finds sitting in the next cubicle. Or meandering with through a maze of cars, to get to the other side of the street, to punch the same time clock. Or the name of the person sitting on the next coffee-shop stool, reading the wants ads, hoping to add another fifty bucks a week to their take-home, so they can keep pace with the rent increase on a one-bedroom, third floor walk-up.

These are working-class names. Names that reek of a heritage of hard knocks. And something else these names have in common? They are the list of the dead. Names that churn working-class mothers' and fathers' guts sour with fear as they lie awake in the night, waiting for the phone to ring, or the door to open. Awake to hear the nerve-easing sound of their daughter's voice. Only then can these parents lower the lids over their bloodshot eyes and squeeze in a few winks of sleep before the 6 AM alarm rings.

Susan Hailey Newcastle was probably a sweet kid. Even if she wasn't, we should think of her in that way. "Never speak ill of the dead," my mother always said. And "Never hold the child responsible for the sins of the parent" was another of my blessed mother's rules.

But in this city partitioned by class, not until the name of the dead reeks of privilege does the indignation of the rich show up. Only in our Reality TV world can a blow-hard like Bradford Lawson wheel out before the camera a middle-aged freelance photographer, (who, my sources assure me, is from a previous life, himself, a Silicon Valley millionaire many times over) who announces the sacrifice of his earnings—earnings garnered from the mortuary shots he's sold to the very newspaper you now hold in your hands—to console the victim's families suffering from who Lawson now denounces as a "Heinous Fiend." A fiend, who until a week ago, had only stuck an ice pick into the skulls of the working class, and not the progeny of the privileged.

Now Bradford Lawson offers a $500,000 reward for the capture of the fiend. An amount of money unimaginable to a working stiff. Bradford Lawson is a man of Enron generosity. He'll figure out some way for his accountants to take the reward money from Lawson Worldwide at the sacrifice of its employees.

Another of my departed mother's words-to-the-wise: "The rich will only do what is good for the rich."

I folded up *The New York Journal*, thinking of Tommy Convoy's mother's Irish wisdom.

I thought of my own departed mother. A tough little Greek woman who had just one wise saying: "Never let anyone shit on you!"

TWENTY-SIX

THE NEW YORK HERITAGE CLUB Events Committee's Save-The-Date card had been mailed long before Bradford Lawson's name was associated with the Fashion Killer murders. Lawson's scheduled talk: Redefining New York City Architecture in the Twenty-first Century. I had him scheduled for a different talk.

All afternoon, the calls kept coming. Members who had sent in regrets were having a change of heart. By 7 PM the guest list had swelled to capacity.

The club's quarterly dinner meetings usually made for a four-line filler in the Metro Section of *The New York Times*. And that was only if someone on the events committee wrote the blurb and called it in to the paper. Now, for the first time in its hundred-twenty-year history, the press, television and radio stations all swarmed the enclosed courtyard outside the club.

A select group, hand-picked by Lawson's staff, were allowed into the main dinner hall. And not even these select few reporters were allowed into the Astor room for the Guest of Honor meet-and-greet.

Beneath the sparkle of century-old Tiffany chandeliers, Lawson had the presence of a man who had never lost a minute's sleep by a troubled conscience. He was relishing his new role of crime-buster, standing conspicuously at the center of the room, shaking hands with men who'd give up their right testicle to be seen on Page Six with him.

My testicles firmly in place, I walked up to the Guest of Honor. Lawson's hand reached out with the perfunctory precision of a flesh-pressing politician. I gripped it tightly. Didn't shake the man's hand. Just held it firm. And kept holding long past what anyone would consider cordially acceptable. Lawson didn't flinch. "How's the big roller?" he asked, tightening his grip against mine.

"You're the one rolling the dice now," I said.

"A half-million bucks will get a lot of gutter rats squealing."

"I wouldn't put my money on a gutter rat holding the key to the Fashion Killer's door."

"No," Lawson squinted. "Then who?"

"A penthouse rat."

"None in my building. Rent is too high."

"We'll see about that. I'm about to fumigate the place."

We released hands as a testicle donator, with a broad smile and hand out, moved up beside us.

I noticed a barrel-chested, middle-aged man in a cheap suit a few feet away, tongue-twirling a wooden toothpick in the corner of his mouth. Lawson's bodyguard.

THE INTRODUCTION OF the Guest of Honor was all accolades for the man, who not only set up a Victims Relief Fund, and put up a reward to catch the killer, but also had, by having Weinberg agree to remove his photographs from publication, set a moral high-bar for the press.

After fifteen minutes of introduction, and another five minutes of standing ovation, Lawson took the podium, and immediately surprised the members of the New York Heritage Club by announcing he was donating land to the city for one dollar. The land to be used for the community park that one of the Young Metropolitans League Benefit dinners had help raised funds to build. "The November dinner," he added, "at which the Fashion Killer had laid claim to a fourth victim. Miss Candice Nolen."

"Miss Nolen's uncle is a member of your club and is here tonight." Lawson looked out from the podium, searching. "Mr. Centaur. Jack, where are you?"

I stood at the back of the room, not about to respond, until one of the other members pointed me out. I nodded towards the front of the room. But not towards the podium.

"I want to add that I have the outstanding architect, Antonio Rizolato, working pro bono on the project," Lawson smiled, all teeth.

Bradford Lawson was going all out to prove himself a humanitarian of the highest order. Rizolato was the preeminent architect of the East Hampton set. I thought of the man's work in the same league as that of Frank Gehry: all glass-and-glint.

A dozen photographers charged forward, shooting pictures from every angle. A Fox News talking head made last-minute touch-ups to her makeup, preparing for a "News at Ten" live feed.

Bradford Lawson's public relations campaign was in full swing. Maybe he believed he could buy the town off. Maybe he believed he could fool all the people all of the time. Whatever it was he believed I didn't give a damn. I believed Lawson was my only hope of finding Candice's killer.

But I'd have to wait. There was no way I'd get Lawson away from his worshippers tonight.

OUTSIDE, THE NIGHT had turned cold. I pulled the collar of my Burberry up to the icy wind and headed in the direction of the East River. I needed to suck in the brisk air of the city to clean my lungs of the stench of bullshit they had sucked in at the club.

The residential streets of Manhattan are naked of citizens on nights as cold as this one was. I passed a breezeway between two well-worn brick apartment buildings, smiling on seeing that there were still some places using the old metal trashcans of my youth. It was just a simple breezeway. Not a dark alley. But it worked just as well for the guy who slugged me.

He had come up from behind. Caught me with a solid kidney punch. Pushed me into the breezeway, pressed my face forward against the hard brick wall. I felt the wet toothpick digging into my cheek as the coward growled, "Stay away from Mr. Lawson." Then I took another kidney punch that buckled my knees.

Spinning sensation. Clouds of random dreams. Candice lying perfectly still on a white tile floor. Shadow of a gingerbread man floats between the translucent pastel glow of twin hollow columns of blue light streaking up from the asphalt, slicing the black sky. An ice pick. A dance floor packed with young people. Again, the gingerbread man. The upper torso and head a shadow. The dough-white cookie legs. I see the phantom of a hand—my hand—reaching out. Grasping for one of the torso's legs. Then, the sensation of smell. The stench of something organic rotting. Still spinning, but slower. Galvanized steel buildings. The spinning now like a slowing merry-go-round taking its final turn. My eyes burn. My tongue tingling back to life the way it does after the dentist has numbed it with Novocain. The galvanized steel morphs into trashcans.

Using the brick wall as a brace, I pull myself slowly, very slowly to my feet. I'm standing. Barely.

I managed a few steps out of the breezeway, my head clearing. For some reason I check my watch. 11:48 PM. In all, it had lasted maybe fifteen minutes. Twenty, at the most. It felt much longer. I had never been KO'd before.

Like a businessman with a few too many under his belt, I swayed on weak legs, hailing a cab to the curb. Later, I knew I was going to have my date with Bradford Lawson. But just then I had a more pressing date with a bottle of Advil.

TWENTY-SEVEN

THE BUZZER DIDN'T WAKE ME. The pounding did.

I crawled out from under the Burberry, stood up and wanted to puke. I stumbled to the door. Squinted through the peephole, then I slid back the dead-bolt lock to let Andy in.

"It's two o'clock in the afternoon. We've got a damn business to run. Where the hell—"

My shirt looked slept-in. My trousers scuffed at the knees. Jacket and tie thrown over a leather recliner. The garbage-stained Burberry I had used for a blanket hung half off the couch. An open bottle of Advil sat on the coffee table. On the floor, its damn childproof cap leaned edgewise against the heel of my upturned Church's wingtip. Three fingers of rust-colored water, once the ice that had cooled my scotch, now melted, sat in a tumbler next to the Advil, completing the picture for my partner.

I limped back toward the couch. Andy put one of his huge hands on my shoulder. I arched in pain.

"Jesus. What hit you?"

"A toothpick."

Andy smirked. "What?"

"It was attached to one of Lawson's goons," I said, bending over the coffee table.

Andy, pushing my jacket and tie aside, planted himself in the recliner, crossed one tree-trunk leg over the other and said: "Talk."

I shook six brown-and-white tablets out from the Advil bottle, swallowing them down with the murk left in the tumbler. I moved the Burberry, sat on the couch opposite Andy and filled him in.

"And the next thing I know," I said, very slowly reaching below the coffee table for my odd shoe, and finding the Advil cap, giving it a crooked twist back onto the bottle, "I'm doing a drunken dance with a couple of garbage cans."

Andy sat calmly. His only movement was the slow, calm, rhythmic tapping of his index finger on the recliner's soft armrest.

Calm on Andy is a very bad sign, like stillness before a hurricane.

"I'll take care of it myself," I said.

"Yeah, right," Andy muttered.

"I mean it. Stay out of this."

"You're starting to worry me, partner. Worry me real bad."

"I can handle it."

"Hey big Medal of Honor winner, you really *are* dreaming if you believe you've still got the right stuff at fifty-six you had at twenty to go after whoever murdered Candice."

I grimaced with pain, moving a pillow behind my aching back.

"This Mr. Toothpick," Andy grunted. "He's a nobody. Just some bum a putz like Lawson keeps around to make him feel like he's one of the *boys,*" Andy bent his nose with a finger. "Lawson's been watching The Sopranos too much."

"Come on. Lawson must have some connections," I said. "He gets construction done around this town when the city can't get a union man to lift a brick."

"He pays off the right people. Believe me nobody owes that creep a favor."

"Good. Then nobody'll care if he gets hurt."

"Not a fuckin' soul. But he's still not your guy. "

"Yeah. So where was the son-of-bitch when his son was trying to call him about a body in a bathroom?"

"Maybe The Brad was taking a shit."

"You've been in a men's room lately?" I laughed, and my lower back took a painful spasm. "A stall is just another office cubicle. Lawson would have answered."

"So what are you saying? Lawson didn't answer Michael's call because he already knew what his kid was calling about?"

"Lookit. I told you Betty had this feeling someone was with Candice when she called that night. Maybe it was Bradford Lawson."

"Come on. You think he was hitting on Candice and she turned him down, so he killed her. That's some long-shot you're betting on, partner."

I shrugged. It hurt. "It's the only shot I've got."

"And what's Lawson's thing?" Andy shook his head. "Converting young lesbians to prove he's the GREATEST cunt man on the planet? And if they don't lay back and see the light? What then, he whips out an ice pick. And for good measure he poses the body for a front-page photo spread so his agency can get bad publicity."

"Okay, so let's say I just want to know where the hell Bradford was from the time Candice left the club until she was found by Virginia. He's got something to do with these murders. I just know it in my gut, Andy. I just know it."

"I'm telling you again. You're in over your head here. You're not a kid anymore. Face it! You're just another fat-ass middle-aged guy whose been living the good life too long. Let it go!"

"Don't tell me who I am." I stood up, adrenaline fighting off the pain. "I've had it with this fucking ugly world we live in. You can't walk the streets anymore without the fear of something. The government haunts us with the fear of terrorists." I pointed now to my window overlooking downtown Manhattan. "I stood right here," I said, my words burning my throat, "looking out this very window, morning tea in my hand, enjoying the crisp clear view of downtown. I can still see it! That antenna on the roof of the North Tower looking like a long sewing needle stuck on the highest fuckin' point in the greatest fuckin' city in the world. And I watched those motherfuckers fly two planes right into the Towers. Stood here watching. I saw that needle hover for an eternal second above a gray-black cloud of toxic smoke before it descended straight down. Didn't need a TV talking head to tell me where Ground Zero was. I've been at the center of too many of 'em.

"And now a maniac is killing innocent girls to instill us with even more fear. Damn it Andy, I was sent off to fight a war for nothing. To fight a war made by old men. So yeah, partner, your right, now it's me who's the old man. But I'm not letting anyone else fight for me. This is the war I'm owed. This is why I had to kill all those others. Enemies, yes! But enemies I had nothing against. Had to kill them so that I'd be ready. Ready to take back my city. Take back my home. And take it back now!"

Andy was still sitting calmly in the chair, watching the spittle run at the corners of his partner's mouth.

I took a deep breath, let it out and said, "Andy, I love you like the brother I never had. But don't get in my way. Please."

Andy rose from the chair. He stood a full head above me. With a grimace of reluctance he pulled something dark and heavy from his coat pocket. "Then take this," he said.

My eyes fixed hard onto what my partner held.

"Unless," Andy said, "you expect to take someone out with your Mont Blanc."

I took the Berretta 9-millimeter pistol strapped inside its black leather back-holster.

"Now don't go blowing your foot off with this gun," my partner said.

THIRTY-FIVE YEARS HAD passed since I had last wrapped my hand around a killing machine.

Andy was wrong when he called it a gun. I could still see the scene in my mind. Basic training. "Grab what you've got between your legs, Soldier." And Private First Class Centaur grabbed himself in the crotch. "Now you sorry-ass piece of shit," the Drill Sergeant barked, "THAT is your gun. That piece of steel you're holding in your other hand. Soldier, THAT is your weapon! Now give me fifty!"

And Private First Class Centaur dropped to the prone and gave the sergeant fifty push-ups.

I knew now, with the cold weight of a weapon back in my hand, I had chosen only one way for this all to end.

I went into my bedroom. To the dresser. Opened the top drawer. Pushed my hand deep into the back—behind the thick, neat row of cashmere socks—and put the 9-millimeter down beside my Medal of Honor.

TWENTY-EIGHT

THE NIGHT WAS AS COLD and icy as the night before, the night I was warned to stay away from Mr. Lawson.

Outside Lawson Grand Tower Apartments, Bradford Lawson walked to the curb. Toothpick waited at the open rear door of a black Lexus. Lawson got in. Toothpick slapped shut the door behind his boss. Eyeing traffic, he walked around the trunk to the driver's side, slid in behind the wheel, and pulled away from the curb. Across Sixth Avenue, I rolled the Jaguar away from the curb.

The Lexus squeezed left, turned west on Fifty-Third Street. Crawled two blocks, then swung south down Seventh Avenue. So did the Jaguar.

Broadway theatres had not let out yet, so Seventh Avenue traffic was light. At Thirty-Ninth Street, Seventh Avenue passes through the Garment District and the street signs change to read Fashion Avenue. It is a hollow part of midtown at night. A manila dress-size tag, fallen off one of the thousand steel dress racks that roll through the avenue during the day, blew up against the Jaguar's windshield. I noticed its shoe-heel-scuffed corner. I felt I was getting too close to the Lexus. I braked. The tag tumbled across the Jag's hood, floated down onto the black asphalt gutter of Fashion Avenue.

At the Northwest corner of Seventeenth Street, the Lexus pulled over. Toothpick remained behind the wheel. The figure of a petite woman, face hidden deep within the fur-lined hood of a dark coat, stepped from a doorway towards the Lexus. Its rear door opened. The woman bent her head forward, got in.

Toothpick made a right onto Seventeenth Street. A right again on Eleventh Avenue. Lexus and Jaguar were now heading north towards the George Washington Bridge.

It seemed Lawson had a little hideaway in the Jersey town of West New York. The Lexus pulled under a covered carport. A sign read: Tenants Only. I pulled the Jaguar to the edge of a construction site across from the carport. I had a full view of the Lexus and the rear entrance to the building that Lawson had walked through with his mysterious cloaked lady. Toothpick lit a cigarette, leaned against the Lexus. When he finished his smoke, he got back into the car and waited. We both waited. An ambush requires patience.

Three hours passed. White vapor spat from the Lexus' exhaust pipe. Lawson must have called Toothpick. A few short minutes passed, and Lawson with his girlfriend, her face still hidden deep within her coat's fur hood, walked all cozy towards the Lexus. Toothpick stood beside the rear door of the car again. Lawson nodded to his flunky. Toothpick gripped the door handle.

I swung a tire iron against the flunky's fat hand. Before Toothpick could let out a scream, I thrust the heel of my left palm into the man's chin. Toothpick's knees buckled. He was down on all fours. I looked to Lawson. The Brad was making a move inside his jacket. *Son-of-a-bitch must be packing.* I pulled back the tire iron and said, "Go for it. I'd love to take your fucking head off."

"Okay Centaur, Okay." Lawson held very still.

I reached inside The Brad's jacket. For a guy who boasted having the "biggest" of everything, I pulled a shining little pussy-pistol out of his waist holster.

I turned to the woman, who hadn't yet uttered a single sound. She lowered her hood, saying, "Hello Jack."

I don't know why I felt disappointed. After all, what the hell did Loretta Devon mean to me?

I stared at her, but spoke to Lawson. "Help up that pile of shit."

"Sure, sure. Just don't go crazy."

Lawson lifted up his soon-to-be-fired bodyguard.

Tire iron in one hand, Lawson's weapon in the other, I nodded for the femme fatale to open the rear door of the Lexus. I ordered them all to slide onto the back seat. Lawson pushed Toothpick onto the seat first and followed his defunct protector in. Devon went to follow, but I changed my mind and said, "No. You, get in the front."

Loretta walked around to the passenger side. Stopped. Stared across the car's roof at me. Slowly she slid down into the shotgun seat.

The rear door still open, I saw the two men. Toothpick was cupping his hand against that barrel-chest of his. Lawson was scared shitless.

I laid the tire iron on the roof, opened the driver's door, and, brandishing the pistol at the boys, slid onto the driver's seat. Loretta's back was pressed against the passenger door. Her eyes piercing me like emerald darts.

Lawson was staring down the barrel of his own weapon. And behind it, me.

My voice a strained whisper falling somewhere between anger and the fear of what I might do next, I said, "Don't anyone be stupid. This is the No-Witness-Left-Behind program. If I'm forced to kill one of you, I have to kill all of you."

"You broke my fuckin' hand. You broke my fuckin' hand."

"Randal, you idiot, shut the hell up." Lawson squealed, his voice braking like a boy in puberty.

So Toothpick had a name.

"Some working over you gave me, Randal. I couldn't piss all night, you son of a bitch," I gritted. "Now zip up your mouth and let's hear what your boss has to say."

"What the hell do you want from me? What's you're problem?"

"Where were you when my niece was killed?"

"You think I killed your niece?"

"Where were you?"

"Jesus, let me think for minute. You don't need to point that gun at me."

"Where were you?"

'Uh..uh…oh yeah..yeah. I had to make some calls. Went outside. Too noisy in the club. Yeah, that's what I did…I made some important business calls."

"You left the club to make some phone calls?"

"That's right."

"So how come your cell phone was off when Michael tried reaching you?"

"It wasn't off. When I'm talking the calls go directly to voice mail."

"The police checked your cell records," I bluffed. "Your phone was off."

"The police! How…"

"He was in my suite."

Lawson flung Loretta a look that told me the woman spoke the truth.

The loyal girlfriend lays out the alibi to save her lover. Her suite was down the hall from Virginia and Michael's. Bradford excused himself from the party guests saying he had some pressing calls he had to make. Fifteen minutes later Loretta left the party, taking the express elevator to the private floor. The kind of floor hotels have that are the equivalent to the VIP section in a club. Bradford was waiting in her suite when she arrived. I questioned the time. Devon said, "Around eleven-forty-five."

"That's when I turned my cell off," Lawson spoke up from the back seat.

"Didn't want anything to break your concentration, huh?"

Lawson let my shot at his mojo slip by. "Well there you are. I'm clean," he said, as if negotiating a deal. "So let's just forget tonight ever happened."

The smug face. The puckered lips. Scumbag knew he was off the hook.

"Okay, asshole," I said. "That still leaves Mikey needing to answer some questions."

"My son! My son was the one who called 9-1-1."

"Your daughter-in-law said she hadn't seen her husband for at least an hour before she went up to the suite. Had no clue where he was.

And then she calls his cell and he beams himself up into the suite like some kind of goddamned Captain Kirk!"

"What do you expect? Ginny says there's a dead body on the floor!"

"Maybe Mikey's close by because he's expecting the call?"

"Stay away from my son!" Lawson leaned an inch forward.

"Fuck you! I already roughed up Mikey once for being an arrogant asshole like his father. Maybe it's time to give him a good working over. Find out what he's hiding."

Lawson's eyes bulged. He leaned forward another inch. If Lawson ever wanted to kill a man, I knew it was me at this moment. But I also knew the buffoon hadn't the balls—just the mouth.

I thought of dropping my guard—give the bastard his chance—when Loretta broke the silence: "Michael was down the hall, in bed with Susan Newcastle."

Lawson turned to her. This was news to him.

"The apple doesn't fall far from the tree?" I grinned at Lawson.

Even in the darkness of the back seat, I could see Lawson's white-bread face turning sunburn red.

"It's an arrangement," Devon explained, glancing over to Lawson, and then looking back to me. "They attended university together at Princeton. They were lovers."

"Then why didn't they marry?" I asked.

"Come home and say he wants a merger with a Newcastle? Daddy's biggest rival. The bane of his existence. Daddy wouldn't like that."

"So he marries someone from the office. Someone neutral."

"Susan obtained the position for Ginny," Devon said.

"You're saying Michael and Susan just give up their relationship. And Susan then offers Ginny as a substitute?"

"Ginny and Susan knew each other since grade school. Before Ginny got expelled. Ginny's a schemer. She needed to rid herself of the society-slut image. She proposed a plan," Loretta sneered. "Michael has a clean image. God only knows how. But he does. Marrying Michael Lawson would give Ginny a clean slate. So she says 'marry me and I'll be your cover.' Michael can hook up with Susan all he liked as long as Ginny has access to the proper society world and has a seat on the board of the Young Metropolitans League."

"Michael's an idiot." Lawson's face turned to disgust. "She's got him by the balls."

"So if Michael wanted to be with Susan Newcastle, Virginia could call all the shots," I said, looking at Lawson. "Pretty shrewd little deal maker you've got there for a daughter-in-law, Bradford."

"I'll say," Loretta said.

"Well, the last I saw of Virginia's lock on that deal it was on its way to the morgue," I said.

"I'll ruin the fat conniving whore!"

"You'd better take good care of Virginia," I said to Lawson. "You don't want Michael's ménage a trois marriage of convenience to make the tabloids."

"She says a word about the Lawson family she gets nothing. There's a prenup."

"Schmuck," I laughed. "The book deal alone will cover what the Lawson prenuptials have been known to piddle out to discarded wives. And who knows what Virginia Kirk-Lawson could get for the movie rights?"

"Ah, it'll all fade away like the Lewinsky thing did," Lawson said, falling back in the seat.

"That was about blow-jobs and cigars," I said. "This story has a serial killer in it. And every corpse has Lawson taint on it."

I looked over to Toothpick hunched in the leather seat, his face pale with pain. Pain I had inflicted. "Who were you in the sack with at the time?" I asked him. "The floor maid?"

Toothpick repositioned his broken hand and winced, "My wife. Boss sent me home early."

Guy's just another working stiff working for a lousy boss.

"Randal," I said, "unless you want to take things to another level, the hand evens us up. Right?"

The poor son-of-a-bitch looked down at the swollen slab of meat lying on his lap and then back to me, the guy responsible, and grunted, "Get the fuck who killed your niece and put one in the fuckin' head for me."

TWENTY-NINE

I DROVE BACK ACROSS THE GW Bridge and through the Manhattan streets in a trance, passing cars that seemed no more than a blur of painted steel, obeying traffic signals by instinct, not by any cognizant thought of their existence.

What kind of people were these? Not an ounce of integrity in any of them. A self-indulgent putz, cheating on his third wife with his daughter-in-law's business partner. His spineless son, raised with a silver spoon in his mouth, so fearing he'd be cut off from the family fortune he makes a deal with the Devil, marries a beast, so he can live in secret with the woman he really loves. And now that woman is dead.

And Loretta Devon? Both her parents dead by the greed of success, she ditches London for a start-up life in Manhattan and falls into the same cesspool of greed she's trying to ditch. I had her figured for more smarts. More class. What could possibly make her bed Bradford Lawson? She'd didn't strike me as a gold digger. And if she was, she had too much intelligence, too much beauty, to have to settle for Viagra sex. There were plenty of rich young men who'd give up their eyeteeth to hear the seductive British whisper of Loretta Devon in the dark of night.

I looked at the age-spotted hands steering the Jaguar—hands that had just mutilated a man. So who was *I* to pass judgment on any of them? Andy was right: I was not twenty years old and in Nam. I was back in The World.

The World. Funny how the mind works. To be thinking in jungle terms just then. *The World.* How many times does a grunt tell himself that when he gets back to *The World,* things will be different? Living for weeks in the same sweat-drenched fatigues, stained red by the clay that permeates that country. Clay that seeps deep into a man's skin.

Like all grunts have in every war since the beginning of time, I made promises to myself. Back in *The World,* I'd never again go a day without a shower. Back in *The World,* I'd go buy the best clothes! Back in *The World,* I'd marry Sharon! Have kids! A nice house!

Yes, I had made promises to myself.

I knew too, that I was luckier than many of the other grunts that did make it back to *The World*; I fulfilled most of those promises. All but one: the one I never had the chance of fulfilling because Sharon was dead before I made it back to *The World.*

It had taken months to wash that red clay of Nam from my skin. With every shower, sometimes two showers, sometimes three showers in the same day, I would watch a little more of the red silt swirl down the drain. Then one day, the water finally ran clear. All the red was gone, and I accepted I was now really back in *The World.* I gave up stalking street gangs, hunting for Sharon's killers. No, The Fashion Killer wasn't my first search-and-destroy mission in this city of unfulfilled dreams.

I learned to live with Sharon's death as I had learned to live with all the other deaths I'd known during my year in Nam. I told myself she was just another number in the body count of my life. I was young. I had the strength. So I grit my teeth, and moved forward into *The World.*

I buried myself in textbooks, in tax laws, in green-lined ledger sheets with long columns. Calculating debits and credits. I liked that at the end of the grueling day, when the books are closed on a company, all the columns must be in balance. Assets minus Liabilities must always equal Equity.

Now, thirty-five years later, I did not fool myself. I knew what Andy said was true: I no longer possessed the stamina of the young. So I knew I needed to choose my shots carefully. There was going to be no second chance.

Deep within those age-spotted hands gripping the steering wheel, I felt the red clay rising again. It had not all washed out. I should have known it would never be all gone. The clay rising made every nerve in me tingle to kill someone. Someone I could see only as a faint cloud in my mind's eye. A free form without details. Yet I knew the form would eventually take shape, and when it did, when it was fully formed, it would be someone connected to Lawson's deceitful, self-indulgent world.

What was the point of such grotesque murders? Was it just some sicko's thrill of seeing women posed on the front page of a newspaper? Or was the killer someone out to destroy Fargo? If so, the plan backfired. Every trust-fund brat in the city wanted to be seen in a Fargo design.

Or was it someone out to ruin Bradford Lawson? Union disputes, tenant strikes, city ordinances violations, near bankruptcy; all failed to destroy him. Maybe a string of dead models would be the dagger to penetrate The Brad's Teflon-coated empire.

I had just held three people at gunpoint. Had sworn to kill all of them if they gave me the slightest reason to do so. In my trance, behind the wheel of my $100,000 Jaguar—yes, I'd been luckier than most other grunts—I asked, *Would I really have killed them?* And the question scared the hell out of me, because I didn't know the answer. All I knew was in the end I would balance the books. And get my equity.

THIRTY

PULLED THE JAG INTO Ace Parking Garage around dawn. It had been a long night. I parked in my rented spot and walked the half-block back to my apartment. The first edition of *The New York Journal* had just hit the street.

It had been three days since Weinberg pulled his photographs from publication. *The New York Journal* had no choice but to go on a righteous editorial bandwagon, agreeing with its star photographer that running the pictures of the victims would only entice more killings.

I nodded to Freddy; he ripped a copy of the paper from the tied stack lying in the lobby and handed it to me. The headline read:

LETTER TO CONVOY: THE NEXT WILL BE MY MASTERPIECE!

I stepped into the elevator. Pressed number twelve. Fumbled in my pocket for my foldaway reading glasses, and pulled open the newspaper.

"At the request of the New York City Police Department," Convoy's page-two article began, "The Journal is withholding from print the actual letter I received from The Fashion Killer. All I can write at this time is that whoever is committing this heinous slaughter of innocent young women has threatened to make the next murder so horrific every paper in the country will be forced to run the picture. The letter promises: 'It will be my masterpiece!'..."

I rushed into my apartment, reached for the telephone and called Dent's cell. Before I could get a word out, Dent said: "Where the hell have you been? I've been calling your place and your cell all night!"

I looked down at the blinking red light on my answering machine, and then over to where my cell phone was still plugged into the battery charger. It wasn't the first time I'd left home without it.

"I want to see the letter."

"No shit, Sherlock! Get your ass over to the Empire Diner."

DENT SAT IN a corner booth at the far end of the Empire Diner. I walked past two construction workers sitting on stools, cajoling across the counter with a bright-eyed waitress. I must have looked as though I needed a strong cup of coffee. The waitress came out from behind the counter and sat one down on the table at the same moment I slid into the booth. A plate of half-eaten sunny-side-ups with home fries lay in front of the detective. "Whadaya have?" the waitress asked.

"Just a glass of ice water, please."

The waitress shrugged, grabbed a plastic pitcher from the setup stand near the booth, poured water into a tumbler, placed it down on the table, and strolled back to join her regulars at the counter. Two thin, melting ice cubes floated in the glass.

Dent busted an egg yoke with a wedge of burnt toast with his right hand; his left pushed a manila envelope across the table saying, "It's a copy. Forensics is going over the original."

I pulled a single sheet of everyday plain white bond paper from the envelope. Dent stuck the yellow soaked toast into his mouth.

I pushed aside the unwanted coffee, swallowed down half of the warm water, and read The Fashion Killer's threat.

Dear Mr. Convoy:

The editors of The New York Journal have taken the position that I'm a heinous fiend. The editors further agree with Mr.

Weinberg's decision not to indulge the "fantasy" of whom "they" have dubbed The Fashion Killer by displaying the photographs of the victims. Should a museum not display Picasso's Guernica because it shows death? I am an artist. A great one! Only a great artist could take a mediocre designer such as Fargo and make his work look marvelous. Alluring. And to do it without supermodels.

Mr. Convoy, you said they are common names: common names to common faces. And now that a young, beautiful socialite has been added to the list of those you see as "victims" and I see as "subjects" the rich have entered the arena.

Bradford Lawson also calls me a heinous fiend. Would Bradford Lawson call me a fiend if he were making millions off me? No! If I made money for him, or if The Brad needed me for his own Machiavellian purpose, he'd hail me in that ingratiating Caesar-hailing-Marc Antony manner he reserves for his sycophant of the moment, as The Greatest! Best Ever! Most Successful! His Close Friend!

It is The Brad who is the heinous fiend. He and his kind. Pompous, self-indulgent fools. All of them.

Susan Newcastle was a warning. My next work will be my masterpiece. A variation on a theme, multiplying the magnificence of my technique.

Now I am called The Fashion Killer. Yet, in time, history will call me an innovator. And those who died? Sacrifices to great art.

The letter was unsigned.

I looked out over my reading glasses. "So what do you make of it?"

The *real* detective followed the last of his eggs with a sip of the garage-brew, wiped his mouth with a paper napkin, crumpled and tossed it onto the empty plate, leaned back in the booth and said:

"Works in the fashion industry. Frustrated by lack of recognition. Knows their way around a sentence. Hates Bradford Lawson, and anyone connected to his world."

"Or envious of him," I said.

"Or rejected by him."

I raised an eyebrow.

"The Brad blows off people just to show he has the power to do it," Dent said.

"A disgruntled employee? Someone he's fired?"

Dent pointed to the letter still in my hand, "Look at that line. 'If I made money for him...'"

I picked up the glass of water. Sipped. My throat was dry and coarse. I had asked a lot of questions this long night, and still had few answers.

Dent shook his head, saying, "Whoever it is—he's not small on ego. Great artist? An *innovator*?"

"Some innovation," I said, putting the glass down. "Ice-picking live models into stiff mannequins."

"It's not an ice pick."

"What?"

"Just a newspaper gimmick. Something I guess they coined to sell papers. Not sure myself who started it."

"So why didn't the police correct them?"

"The department doesn't comment on ongoing investigations," Dent smiled.

"Riiiight. Don't want to tip off the perp."

"Perp. Listen to Detective Centaur, will ya?"

"Okay. Okay. Just tell me what the hell it is then?"

"A surgically sharp needle of some kind. About as thick around as a knitting needle. Not very long, though. Maybe as long as one of those...what's it called?"

"A crocheting needle?"

"Yeah, as long as a crocheting needle. Only has to go about three inches up into to the base of the neck, penetrate the brain. Instant death."

"A quick and clean kill," I muttered.

"What?"

"Nothing." I shook my head. "Must have some kind of medical background to figure out just where to stick this needle."

"Or checked it out on the Internet. Hell, these days any nut can learn how to make a nuclear bomb online. Anyway, like I told you, whoever it is, he or she knows the victim. Remember, no signs of forced entry. No bruises on the victim indicating a struggle. In fact, the angle of entry indicates the killer is facing the intended victim and reaching around." Dent curved his arm out, his hand clenched. "Kind of like when someone reaches around to hug you. Then the killer plunges the needle up into the base of the brain. Dead in an instant. Victim never knows what hit her."

"Hmm..."

"What?" Dent asked.

"Well...I never considered the killer for a woman."

I had had nights when I'd woken up soaked in a nightmare-sweat because I'd taken down The Fashion Killer. A man. But what if the Fashion Killer was a woman? I wondered now if I could take a woman down. I wondered would I hesitate? I knew in combat, a soldier had only a split-second to decide: friend or foe, kill or don't kill. Hesitate longer than a split...well, anything longer a soldier didn't have to think about. He'd be dead.

"Man or woman makes no difference to me as long as I get to slap a set of steel cuffs around their guilty wrists," Dent said, as if reading my mind.

"What the hell's this shit about?" I peered down through my glasses, reading out loud: "*A variation on a theme, multiplying the magnificence of my technique.*"

"Going to take down more than one this time."

"Multiple murders?"

"What else could it mean?" Dent asked.

My lips pressed together, I said nothing.

"But I'll tell you this," Dent continued. "Just because the previous murders have occurred right after one of these society kids' fundraisers doesn't mean the next one will. Whoever this Fashion Killer is, they are as hot as hell at Bradford Lawson for making a deal with Weinberg to pull the photographs."

"It was my plan. And that makes me the one responsible to stop him, or *her* from killing again," I said.

"Yep, you dealt those cards, alright. You've certainly done well pushing your sorry amateur ass in this far, and now I'm forced to have you push it in even further. There's no way I can put a detective on the tail of every kid wearing a damn Fargo dress. You're going to have to really penetrate this brat pack, and right now, if we hope to have any chance of catching the bastard before we have another front-page spread. It's a long shot that you'll come up with anything, but you're in this all the way now and I can't stop you." Dent paused. Took a deep inhale, let the breath ease out through his nostrils. "And I don't want to stop you."

Well, the cards were all out on the table now. And I was about to go all-in, playing the hand I had dealt myself out to the very end the same way I had been be playing them all along—by instinct and anger.

"Remember our deal," Dent said, as if again seeing into the mind of the man sitting across from him. "You get close, you call me. We do it by the book."

"Unless it's self-defense," I reminded Dent.

"Riiight."

THIRTY-ONE

THE HOTEL VICTORY HELD COURT to a discreet clientele. So discreet, the management would never consider intruding on their privacy by installing surveillance cameras. After all, *their* guests weren't riff-raff. So I could only imagine the scene of Candice walking down the corridor chatting on her cell, telling her mother she'd be home soon—a car was waiting. All the time, a friend, an acquaintance, a man, maybe a woman, may have been walking alongside her. The person had to have met her on the floor because Benny said he had walked Candice to the express elevator. He said he was positive no one else had gotten in with her, and the elevator went directly to the private floor. Which meant whoever murdered her knew she was on her way up to change. But how did they know? And how did the killer come to have access to the floor? The elevator required a VIP suite key to get off at that floor. If the killer wasn't one of the guests with a suite, how'd they get onto the floor? Only three huge suites made up the entire floor. Michael and Virginia had one suite, Bradford Lawson had one, and Loretta Devon had the third. If my hostages had told me the truth, they were too busy between the sheets to be out of their rooms.

I was stuck. Devon said Michael Lawson was on the floor below with Newcastle, so how could he possibly have gotten up to the suite so fast? He'd given his VIP suite key, the key he'd need to access the floor, to Candice. Yet, according to Virginia, Michael was at her side in "like less than 2 minutes."

So the kid must have taken the steps. But private floors in all hotels have security doors, with an alarm that is tripped if someone tries to enter the floor from the stairwell. Even if in the panic of hearing his secretary was dead in his suite Michael had used the steps, and had pushed open the door, he would have set off the alarm and hotel security would surely have hit the floor within the time Michael wasted before he called 9-1-1.

I chewed all this over in my mind while wandering back home from the Empire Diner through Washington Square Park. I found myself entering my apartment for the second time that morning, and it was only 9:30 AM.

I had hit that wall of exhaustion I knew all too well, where my brain just stops functioning. God? How long has it been since I last slept? They still make that Geritol stuff "more iron than a pound of calf's liver." Jesus, I'm getting punchy. I need something for my "Tired Blood."

I opened my refrigerator's freezer and pulled out the pint of Brooklyn Ice Cream Company Chocolate-Chocolate Chip I hoard like a junkie's fix.

SEEMED THE ONLY way I woke up lately was with either a pounding on my apartment's door or the drilling ring of my cell phone. Reaching for my cell on the nightstand, I just missed knocking over a half-pint of chocolate-chip soup.

"Jack, this maniac has gotten me really scared. What's he going Al Qaeda now? Threatening to kill more of Lawson's kind."

"Hello Benny," I groaned.

"Everyone's wondering who's going to be next? What could be more horrific?"

"Calm down, Benny."

"Downs says The Fashion Killer is out to reek havoc amongst the dilettantes."

"Benny," I said, pulling my self up in the bed, "don't go hysterical on me. People are always squawking about something and they're usually wrong."

"But Downs knows."

I looked at the clock. It was 6:45 PM. "Benny, I'm tired. Why'd you call?"

There was a silence from Benny's end, then, "Jack, you do know who Sally Downs is?"

"Sally Downs? The astronaut?"

"That's Sally Ride!"

"Okay Benny, tell me already, will ya?"

"Jack, you gotta get with it. The *Journal's* for the masses. Sally Downs' blog is for the Cipriani Set."

"Never heard of her."

"Well she's heard of you!"

"What are talking about? I never met this Downs broad."

"Broad. You're like so Sinatra," Benny sighed. "You must have seen her. She shows up everywhere."

"Doesn't ring a bell."

"Get out of here. You must have noticed her at the Gala. You notice all the queers. Tallish. Flame red hair. Butch-cut. A dyke, Jack."

"Yes, at the crap table. Gave me a real good bitch-stare."

"That's Sally Downs alright."

"So what! I didn't speak to her."

"Are you kidding me? Bloggers don't do interviews. They do gossip. Innuendo. Good shit. Facts—borrrring!"

"Benny, I'm tired."

"Listen, darling. I've got a piece of info for you."

"Well, give it to me."

"Michael Lawson tried to kill himself."

"What? When?"

"It's all hush-hush. Sometime this morning. Early, maybe four, five o'clock. His mother's place."

"How do you know?"

"*They* may be trying to keep it quiet. But *I* have my contacts."

"You've got someone inside the first Mrs. Lawson's place?"

"Jack, I don't kiss and tell. But believe me my source is solid."

"Benny, you're beautiful. Remind me to *kiss* you."

"Paleeease. You're a bit too long in the tooth for me."

"Where are they keeping Michael?"

"He's still with Mommy. And Mommy is pissed. Blames it all on her ex. Seems Daddy and son had a big fight in the middle of the night."

"Michael was at his mother's?"

"He's been sleeping there ever since Susan was…" Benny paused. "Was found."

"Why?"

"Well, he was having an affair with Susan. Keeping it a big secret from Daddy and all."

"I know about the affair. Michael was in Susan's hotel room when Candice was murdered."

"Now I'm impressed," Benny said. "Even among the brats their affair was one *very* well-kept secret."

"So, Daddy found out?" I asked, not letting on that I was the reason Bradford Lawson was so pissed.

"I don't know exactly what was said, but Daddy burst into his ex's and pulled Michael right out of bed. Strong words and plenty of threats by Daddy to cut the kid off. Even talked of firing his own son.

"That SOB is not one to be sensitive. His kid's lover murdered and this beast doesn't have any compassion. I mean, how could someone? Well, I guess that was enough to put Michael's depression into a tailspin. He took a mouthful of sedatives.

"Mommy went into Michael's bedroom to make nice-nice and found her baby just in time. Good thing the Park Avenue types have their own private doctors on call. Pumped Michael's stomach, or whatever it is they do when a rich kid attempts suicide. These Rolls Royce doctors got the routine down. By God, they see this shit all the time. Anyway, Michael will be okay. Physically that is. He really did love Susan, you know."

"Not enough to show the balls to stand up to his father and marry her in the first place."

"Don't forget," Benny said. "She had a father, too."

"Another winner?"

"Paleeease! The Newcastle-Lawson feud has been going on since like forever."

I rubbed my eyes. My brain was functioning again. "Benny," I said, "I need your source to ask Michael how he managed his way up to the suite so fast after Virginia called."

"He's really not a bad kid, Jack."

"Yeah. Yeah."

"He's fucked up alright," Benny allowed. "But nothing more than spoiled rich. Michael would never have had anything to do with Candice's death."

"I know, Benny. I know. But however Michael got onto that private floor, it's the same way The Fashion Killer did."

"I'm really scared, Jack. Not for myself. For these kids."

So BENNY WANG was getting it on with one of Lawson's ex-wife's household staff. Whoever his boyfriend was, I hoped he could get to Michael before The Fashion Killer decided to get the creative urge again.

I stood in my underwear, looking into the bathroom mirror, wishing I had listened more to my own doctor about cutting down the cholesterol intake and getting in some exercise. I wasn't sure how much longer I'd be able to keep up the fast pace I was running. No, I wasn't a kid anymore. And I shit-sure knew I wasn't Superman, either. Used to be taking a prophylactic meant to me not forgetting to bring a condom along. Now all it meant was remembering to take three Advil before I attempted any strenuous activity.

I shook out a half-dozen of the brown-and-white capsules, choking them down without water. I showered, shaved, and slipped into a fresh shirt, suit and tie. Grabbed my cashmere topcoat and started to head out into the night. Then, reaching for the doorknob, I paused. I decided I had better take one more prophylactic—the 9-millimeter kind.

THIRTY-TWO

MAYBE THERE WAS SOMETHING SUBCONSCIOUS to it—Benny had called them the Cipriani set—that I found myself walking back through Washington Square Park, in the direction of West Broadway, and Downtown Cipriani. I had called Maria's cell after leaving my place. She was home in her sweats, on the couch, rewinding the TiVo. Cipriani was two blocks from her apartment. I asked her to slip on something sexy and meet me for dinner. "I need you with me tonight," I had said. "Give me forty-five minutes," was all she said.

I was passing the Apple Store on Spring Street. It was almost closing time. I stepped inside.

A pencil-thin young man wearing a black T-shirt with the bitten Apple logo walked up to me, brightly smiling, "Can I help you?"

"No thanks, I'm just browsing."

The iMac pulled up Downs' blog in a flash.

The layout and guests were the same, but this was no New York Times Style section. The redheaded dyke was a society tattletale. A piranha feeding on the flesh of the rich. No wonder she was so chummy with the Baxter twins at Club Faux Pas. They were all players in the same world. A world made more decadent by an insatiable voyeur's black hole in need of content. A hole, I was about to learn, where anyone is but one serendipitous mouse-click away from sinking down.

The party pictures were sharp digital shots, annotated by cutting blurbs insulting the Lawsons, Newcastles and every other socialite who attended The Young Metropolitans League event.

Bloggers never need to worry about a nervous editor deleting the libelous stuff. Or the profanity.

The picture was taken outside the ladies room, while I was giving Maria hell for wearing the Fargo. The caption above it read: Uncle Jack Loves Date's Fargo. Orders Fucking $5,000 Exclusive!

How Downs had gotten the shot, or that she had concocted exactly the opposite of what we were talking about didn't bother me. In fact, I thought it would work to my advantage. I wanted the world to know I had consigned the exclusive design. What did bother me though, were the *Journal's* front-page photographs of the victims on the blog. The pictures were not as sharp as the party pictures. They were grainy. Downs must have scanned them directly from the newspaper. *Wasn't this against the law? Wasn't she violating Weinberg's copyright? Couldn't Irwin sue? Get an injunction?* I figured Weinberg probably had his lawyer moving on shutting down the blog. What did it really matter? I knew, and the editors at the *Journal* and Tom Convoy knew, that by the time Weinberg could shut down the blog, The Fashion Killer would have struck again.

"We're closing," the thin kid in the black shirt said. I left the Apple store.

It was a brisk New York night. Standing on the corner of Spring Street and West Broadway, a black musician, wearing a worn wool topcoat and torn jeans, blew Harlem Nocturne through a saxophone, its brass patina catching the reflection of moonlight on every down-beat. The notes resonated along the cannon of West Broadway as I walked to Cipriani. The asphalt gutter reflecting a black glow under the cold white light of the streetlamps, the sidewalks bustling with a mix of starving artists and the well-to-dos.

A slim, well-dressed middle-aged woman with just enough makeup to tone down the crow's feet around her eyes, yet not enough to hide them, stepped from the door of Prada dangling a small shopping bag from her well-manicured, bejeweled hand. A twenty-something sales girl wearing too much makeup, locked the door behind her last commission. The slim woman granted me a tight-lipped smile when I stopped, offering her the courtesy to cross in my path. Her chauffeur waited alongside a double-parked blue BMW 721E. I watched her continue on to the curb with the self-assured strides of a person accustomed to being catered to. She slid into the back seat and I felt a sudden uneasiness in the pit of my stomach. I chalked it up to my conscience telling me I should be meeting *this* woman for dinner, and *not* a kid less than half my age.

I reached the entrance of Cipriani and saw Maria crossing West Broadway in a black leather coat accented by a faux-fur trimmed collar. When this quest of mine was over, I promised myself to buy the kid a mink.

Maria's stiletto heels clicked on the concrete with youthful energy. I held the door to Cipriani open for my date.

No matter the night or the time, Cipriani is always busy. I ate there two, three nights a month. Always alone. Always without a reservation. Always seated without waiting.

"Good evening Mr. Centaur," the maître de smiled. "Please, this way."

He led us to a table near the front window looking out over the patio, where, on a warmer night, the most precious high-profile side-walk tables would be placed.

"May I have the beautiful lady's coat?"

"Thank you, no. I'm a little cold." Maria said, with a shivering gesture.

The maître de held out a chair for Maria, placed two menus down on the table and bowed. "Bon appetite."

A skinny young man with Mediterranean good looks and speaking in the kind of emphasized Italian-waiter accent only spoken inside New York restaurants asked, "A bottle of Pellegrino for the table?"

I told him tap water.

"Something from the bar?"

Maria ordered a Corona, and I a double Chivas on the rocks.

The waiter bowed and said, "Very nice," and headed off to the bar.

"So what's the plan, Jack?" Maria didn't mince words.

"I'm not sure yet. But whatever the plan, I'm throwing it into high gear tonight at the Club Faux Pas," I said, thinking of Dent's urging me to move fast. "Look, I need you to play your role again. By now the crowd knows I'm just some old jerk after a little young stuff. No one will be paying any attention to me."

"You think that the Fashion Killer is going to hit someone at the club tonight?"

"The letter reads like it's going to happen soon. And I can't think of a better place to start out."

"No one has seen the letter but the police."

The waiter returned with our drinks, and with that annoying phony accent.

"Allow me to tell you about our wonderful specials tonight."

"Later," I said, my eyes on Maria.

"Very good," the waiter said, bowing off, annoyed that his customer had broken his soliloquy that always began with "Tonight the chef will prepare for you…"

"You saw the letter!"

I picked up the Chivas.

"How?"

"I can't tell you."

Maria pushed a wedge of lime down the Corona's bottleneck. I watched it settle to the bottom, then whispered, "Pretty sure it's going to be a double murder this time."

Maria's slender, manicured thumb still pressed to the top of the bottle, she gave her boss a *how-can-you-say-so* smirk.

I stared back at her.

"The letter?"

"Maria, I'm just working by gut instinct. It's crazy, I know, but I've got to play the hand out."

"A man's gotta do what a man's gotta do," Maria chided.

"You're not old enough to have seen Shane."

"When a girl's laid up for six months in a body cast, she gets to watch a lot of old movies on the Turner channel."

On Maria's fifteenth birthday she fell off the back of a Harley Davidson. Doctor said she'd never walk the same again. Doctor didn't know Maria. When the cast was removed, she hobbled into physical therapy. And from there into the gym. She hadn't missed a day's workout since.

"Say it anyway you want, Maria. But yeah, I gotta do what I gotta do, is close enough."

"And you think the Fashion Killer is going to be at Faux Pas tonight."

"Just taking a shot," I said. "You got a better idea?"

"Yeah," she said, lifting the bottle of Corona to take a sip, then placing the bottle down firmly in front of her. "Go home."

I waved for the waiter. "Let's eat."

THIRTY-THREE

ELEVEN PM AND THE LINE outside Club Faux Pas was just as long as the last time. And once again Bald Ernie held up the velvet rope for Maria. And once again, I tagged along.

Inside: same scene, different night.

Justin up in the VIP section holding a Coors Light surrounded by the same gaggle of girls. Everyone shouting over the din to speak words no one else cared to hear. A world of shouters empty of listeners. Was I the only one who noticed a void left behind by the absence of a long, blond ponytail, jutting out the back of a black baseball cap with a bright orange P on the front? A void I now added to the debt.

The falcon in a tuxedo opened the gate to the privileged area. This time there were no introductions. Maria squeezed into Justin's group to do a little reconnaissance. I swirled the ice in my second double Chivas of the evening, leaned against the back wall, feeling the press of my weapon nested in its leather holster on the small of my back, and waited. My eyes panning the jungle spread out before me with the intensity of a combat soldier alert for any hint of the enemy's position.

Maria returned from her mission.

"They're all hung up talking about Michael Lawson. Rumor goin' 'round he's real sick. Held up at his mother's place. That Virginia ain't even with him."

Still scanning the floor, I said, "Too many sleeping pills."

"Oh-My-God! What the fuck *don't* you know?"

I stared down at her.

"Yeah, and when you get that figured, then what?"

"I'll call a cop," I lied.

"Gimme a fuckin' break…" Maria wasn't buying my BS.

"How about taking your coat off," I said, wanting to change the subject, my eyes still panning the jungle. "You can't possibly be cold now, not with all the body heat in this place."

Maria bit her bottom lip and removed the coat.

"God damn it!" I cursed myself for not remembering to take the Fargo outfit with me when I rushed from Maria's place the morning Dent called about the Newcastle murder. "Why didn't you give that thing back to Loretta? Or dumped in the garbage, where it belongs?"

"I had a feeling I'd find a use for it again," Maria slyly said.

I took a nervous sip of the Chivas, telling myself: Damn it! I'm going too far now. But I can't turn back. She was the one who put on the Fargo dress. Hell, she's a grown woman. She made her choice. So be it!

I felt a vibration. Pulled my cell from inside my jacket. Couldn't make out the words, but knew the voice.

"Benny, I can't hear you. Give me a minute." I looked to Maria and said. "Going to the men's room. Don't move from here."

I rushed down to the corner of the VIP section and into the men's room. It looked like the inside of a mobile phone store; there were so many men with Bluetooths growing from the side of their heads.

"Okay, Benny I can hear you now," I shouted.

Benny was speaking in a high-pitched staccato of nervous excitement. "My friend says Michael says there's this universal code that is used on a box near the door so emergency people can enter the floor from the stairwell."

"How'd Michael get the code?"

"Thank God my friend thought to ask. I would have died if he didn't."

"Come on, Benny!"

"Okay. Okay. One of the bouncers at Club Faux Pas. They're all part of hotel security, you know. And get this, it wasn't the first time

Michael had used the room. He and Susan had their little tête-à-têtes whenever there was a benefit or private party."

"Who, Benny?"

"What?"

"This bouncer got a name?"

"Cutter. Guy's name is Cutter."

"Thanks Benny. You did great. Now go get yourself a hot toddy and some sleep."

I rushed back to Maria. She hadn't moved. Two, tall skinny young men with half a tank on were hitting on her. "Beat it boys," I growled.

"Didn't know you brought your father," one of them said to Maria. And then they both flipped me the bird in unison and left.

"Which bouncer is Cutter?"

"Cutter?" Maria looked at me as if I should have known. "The guy wearing the tux."

"Come with me."

The falcon had a name: Cutter. I had to stretch my neck up to speak into his ear. "Got to talk to you," I said.

I felt the sting of Cutter's breath mints against my face as he spoke. "Mister, I don't talk to the customers."

"You gave Michael Lawson the security code."

Cutter pulled his head back. Shot me a don't-go-fucking-with-me hard-ass stare.

Maria caught the stare and shouted up to Cutter. "He's good people. He's my boss."

"Your boss?" Cutter seemed confused, then, "He Andy's partner or somethin'?"

"Exactly," Maria shouted over the din.

Cutter cocked his head, broke into a broad smile and said, "Hell, why didn't you say you was Andy's man in the first place."

He signaled to a clone of himself, saying, "I need ten."

The clone took over the bouncer's position by the gold rope.

We followed Cutter through a narrow pantry into a two-by-noth-ing maintenance room. An upright Hoover stood between Cutter and Maria. My left shoulder rubbed against steel shelving stuffed with loose rolls of toilet paper.

"What can I do," Cutter cocked his head, "for Andy's partner?"

I didn't bother, not even for a New York second, to consider in what life Andy and Cutter had traveled together. I already knew Andy Smoothe could leave his highbrow friends, sipping from their flutes of champagne in the lobby of the Metropolitan Opera, and within a half-hour, he'd be shooting craps with hipsters in the back room of a gin mill somewhere in Hell's Kitchen. All that mattered now was, if Cutter knew Andy was my partner, Cutter wasn't going to be handing me any bullshit.

"Who else besides Michael Lawson did you give the door code to the VIP floor?"

Cutter pursed his lips, seeming to consider where I had gotten my information, then answered, "Nobody."

"Cutter, it was my niece they found up in that bathroom."

"Shit, I'm sorry 'bout that. Didn't know. Sorry man, real sorry. But you knows I wouldn't lie to Andy's man. I gave the code to nobody. Truth!"

"Cutter, she was killed by someone who knew that code. I'm sure of this."

"You ain't saying it was one of us. Hey man, every security person works for the corporation has to know the code. Got to, in case we need to evacuate the place." Cutter shrugged. "Anyways, ain't like the code's no big secret or somethin' inside the house. Y'know what I mean. Even housekeeping have it."

"Why'd you give it to Michael? It wasn't for money. Maria tells me you guys can't be bought."

"Michael Lawson's not so bad. Anyways, not the first time he'd be sneaking between them floors. You ever meet that man's wife? Shit, I'd need to be five floors away from her mouth just to get some sleep."

"So almost anyone could get the code?" I asked.

"Y'know, I ain't saying we just give it out. Really, Andy's man, I just gave it to Michael because he does the right thing by me when his friends start getting rowdy."

Cutter grinned at Maria. "He don't go squeezing no gonads, but he sure give them dudes a bad-ass look like he's going to, and they calm down. Yeah, Michael Lawson, he's okay."

"Look, Cutter. You remember anything, anyone comes to your mind who doesn't seem kosher, you call me!"

It seemed my cell number was going out to everyone lately.

"You out to get the dude ain'tcha?" Cutter didn't wait for an answer. "Shit, I shoulda figured that out right away. You being Andy's partner and all."

A LITTLE PAST midnight the Baxter sisters made their entrance.

Same shit-fly entourage swarming about them, the sisters waved and pranced across the dance floor, flaunting their tits and asses like Eleventh Avenue whores working a Javits Center business convention, their ensembles unmistakably Fargo.

Trisha wearing a sleek, sleeveless black satin dress, hemmed six inches above her knees. Two strands of heavy black beads hung from her neck down to her pelvis, her left wrist wrapped inside a four-inch-wide silver slave bracelet. She was stockingless.

Collette's was a low cut, strapless job, just as black, and just as short as her sister's Fargo. The sleeves pushed up to her elbows, a series of thick, chain-link gold bracelets wrapped her pencil-thin forearms; on her legs, coarse black fishnet stockings.

Collette had dyed her hair jet-black and had it ironed straight. And tonight, Trisha's hair seemed even more platinum blond than I had remembered it.

Cutter pulled up the gold rope. The twin's long subtle legs taking slow, stretching strides, up the three steps. Strapped on their feet, the same kind of stiletto-heeled Pradas Candice had worn.

I mashed my teeth. Had someone dared the twins to dress in a fashion to kill?

A glint of red caught my peripheral vision. Then it was gone. I scanned the dance floor, across to the bar, and back again. There!

Again! A flicker of red as quick as a sniper dissolved, melding with the jungle of faces.

Again, I trained my eyes on the mass of bobbing heads. One minute, two minutes. A head swayed and I saw the red glint for a third time. Now I was sure the red was staring back at me. Another head moved. Gone again. I squeezed past the Baxter twins, down the three VIP steps and onto the dance floor. Somewhere out there, Sally Downs was hunting me.

I figured whatever the redheaded dyke saw of me would find its way into her blog by morning. I didn't care. Right then I was more concerned with the goings on in the VIP section. I turned away from the dance floor and went back to join the trust-fund brats.

"I'll have a Vaaacha and Taahneek?" Trisha said, turning an otherwise declarative sentence into a question.

I had felt it earlier that night, seeing the middle-aged woman carrying the shopping bag, and now that butterfly pang hit my stomach again. Something about the Prada shoes? Something was not in the right column!

Maria touched my arm.

"You okay?"

"Yeah, I'm fine."

"You looked like you left the planet there for a minute."

"What happens when this place closes? Where does everyone go? "

"Me, I go home to get some sleep. You forget? I've got a job."

"How about the Baxter girls? Where you figure they'd go?"

"Probably one of those no-name bars downtown. The kind of place, if they ever hung a sign outside, it'd stop being hip and close down in a week." Maria shrugged. "But who the hell knows? The rich bitches could book it to one of their little hideaway pads they have around town."

"Then what?"

"Party some more. Get laid. Whatever. I ain't never been invited, y'know what I mean."

Maria now nodded toward the Baxters.

Trisha's porn-famous long tongue was deep into her cocktail glass stirring the ice, while Mr. Coors Light slowly stroked his crotch, purporting to be inflicted with elephantiasis.

"Anyways," Maria said, turning to me. "I wouldn't go if I was invited. Not my style."

"You've got too much class," I smiled. "Y'know what I mean."

Maria blushed. It looked good on her.

"Come on, let's dance," I said.

"You gotta be kiddin' me."

I was feeling paranoid that I may have been acting more like a cop than the silly old fool I was supposed to be. So we hit the dance floor. I bobbed. I weaved. Showed some overbite. And removed any doubt that I was anything but an old fart fool.

People danced around us. Up against us. In our faces. The music blared. I had the sensation of spinning on an amusement park ride. Feet shuffled, legs stretched. Shoes. Shoes. *Why did my mind keep coming back to shoes?*

I looked up. In the VIP section a commotion was stirring. Collette flailing her arms at one of the women in her entourage, while another woman stood between Trisha and a T-shirt-clad young man. Two more of the group got into the twin's faces. Cutter and his clone moved in and the scuffle died down. Trisha was steaming, the toe of her Prada tapping furiously against the floor.

I had stopped dancing, frozen on the ride.

"What is it?" Maria asked.

"Gotta make a call! Keep your eyes on the Baxters."

I pushed my way through of the dance floor, looking back over my shoulder at the VIP section. Finally, inside the relative quiet of the men's room, I scrolled through my cell phone's received calls, found the number I wanted and pressed call.

After the beep I said, "It's Centaur. Call me as soon as you get this. I need your help."

I hung up, hoping Weinberg would return my call as fast as he did when I had emailed him that very first time.

I elbowed my way back through the crowd. Reached the steps of the VIP section and my stomach dropped. The entourage had lost their idols. The Baxters had vanished.

I turned to Cutter. "What happened?"

"Twins ditched the crew. Blew outta here."

I scanned the VIP section. "Where's Maria?"

Cutter looked around, shrugged. "Don't know."

I pushed through the dance floor crowd like a blitzing linebacker. Jumped out into the street, my testicles up in my throat, heart pounding like a jackhammer against my chest. Headstrong Maria had done her job too well. She had worked herself into an invitation to the Baxter's next partying hole.

Two rings…three rings… In the brisk night air, gripping my cell phone, I felt a cold sweat in my palm. Four rings….five rings…finally hearing Maria's voice I began, "Where the hell—" It was only her voicemail. My eyes panning Tenth Avenue, hoping she'd materialize from the concrete, I waited for the voicemail's beep. My mouth dry, I managed a panicked plea: "Call me, Call me. Get your ass away and call me."

2 AM. Alone, my mind racing, thinking what have I done? Thinking, how in hell am I ever going to find Maria in a city with a million holes to hide in?

I hailed a cab. Headed for the Ace Parking Garage. On the way, I called the one person I knew who could narrow down the number of holes.

THIRTY-FOUR

I TURNED THE JAGUAR ONTO Christopher Street feeling like Don Quixote going after windmills. And then, there, waiting on the stoop of his apartment building, I saw my Sancho Panza, all decked out in red leather.

Benny squeezed between the bumpers of two parked cars, pulled open the shotgun door of the Jag, and before his ass touched the seat, said, "Let's try Little Branch."

"Is this a pop quiz?"

"Oy," Benny sighed. "Eleventh Avenue and First Street."

I hit the gas pedal. Benny scrambled to find the seat belt, blurting, "In one piece, please."

I cut the Jag through the maze of Greenwich Village streets, challenging caution-yellow traffic lights just before they turned red. Benny, all ten fingers pressed white against the dashboard, was too frightened to say anything more than OHMYGOD as pedestrians flipping middle fingers dodged out of harm's way.

"That's it!" Benny pointed to a blood-maroon door, stuck into a grimy gray-white brick façade jutting out like a bruised big toe from the corner of Eleventh Avenue and First Street. "That's Little Branch."

"When did the Board of Health condemn the joint?"

"You're in for a shock, Big Daddy."

"Hell, they could be feeding rats to tomcats perched on barstools for all I care, as long as we find Maria safe inside."

I parked the Jag next to a fire hydrant and took my chances it wouldn't be towed.

No velvet rope to cross, just a bouncer inside the door who Benny knew.

Benny was right: I *was* surprised. The place was a palace: chandeliers and silk drapery and black leather banquettes running along the wall opposite a long black marble-topped bar. The marble polished to a Narcissus-sheen so the patrons could stare at their reflections.

Three male bartenders dressed like palace servants in Aladdin-bloused white silk shirts and red spandex pants were whipping, shaking, blending and doling out fresh fruit-and-alcohol concoctions in tall glasses at twenty bucks a throw.

Benny double air-kissed his way through the crowd with the deft of a Broadway diva. I stood out like a father searching for his runaway daughter.

No one had seen the Baxter posse.

The Jag hadn't been towed.

"Let's try Beebe's," Benny said. And before I could ask, Benny frowned: "Twenty-Seventh between Ninth and Tenth."

This time the bar was leather, and couches instead of banquettes lined the wall. The crowd: long-legged dykes in motorcycle gear and a smattering of voyeur straights. Benny proved he could mix with anyone. He worked the room with a little less air-kissing and a lot more vamping. No one had seen the twins.

It was closing in on 3:30 AM. The bars would shut their doors in thirty minutes.

I checked my voice mail even though my cell didn't indicate a missed a call.

Nothing. Why wasn't Maria calling back? After all, wasn't that why she tagged along with the Baxters in the first place—to be my point man? *What was taking her so long? Was it over? Had the Fashion Killer already made good on the promise, and then some?* I threw the thought from my mind and focused on my mission.

Why hadn't Weinberg returned my call? Maybe he was waiting for another call, the one from his snitch in Dent's Office. I figured it had to be someone close to Dent, someone in the precinct, a person who could give Weinberg the heads up as soon as the Fashion Killer's call came in. Before the call hit the police band, or whatever it was the paparazzi monitored.

Outside Beebe three young women huddled tightly, ohmygod-ding over a cell phone. I heard someone say Trisha. I leaned in, mocking, "Ohmygod, is that the Baxter sisters?"

The girls looked up at the crazy old guy hanging over their shoulders. The one holding the phone said: "My sister emailed it. She just saw them going into the Inn on Eighteenth."

"I should have known," Benny cried. "The rooftop suite is one of their favorite hideaways."

I ran to the Jag. Benny panted behind.

Benny reached once more for the shotgun door.

"You better catch a cab home," I said.

"What?" Benny coughed, trying to catch his breath.

"Thanks for everything. I'll take care of the rest on my own."

"No way."

"Benny, we haven't got time to argue. Go home, and thank you. Really. Thank you very much."

"But…"

"Go home, Benny."

The little man exhaled a long, deep sigh.

I slid in behind the wheel. Looked again over to Benny Wang standing at the curb, knowing the little guy had been ready to go all the way with me. *Damn tough soldier,* I thought, slamming the gas pedal to the floor.

THIRTY-FIVE

I RAN THE JAG'S TIRES up against the yellow-lined curb in front of The Inn on Eighteenth Street. A doorman dressed like he was waiting to join up with his marching band rushed around to the driver's side. My feet hit the asphalt before Major Fife's hand found the car's door handle.

"Checking in, Sir?"

"Checking someone out." I slipped a fifty into the man's palm. "Watch the car."

"Very good, sir," Major Fife said, sounding as if he'd learned his phony British accent from a P.G. Wodehouse novel.

The Inn on Eighteenth Street was the smallest, yet most elite, boutique hotel in the Baxter clan's chain. Only five floors—each one a separate suite for one well-heeled client willing to fork over twenty grand a night. The rooftop suite went for a hundred grand. Must have been a slow booking night, I thought, if the Baxter twins were crashing there. If they died there, I wouldn't be surprised if the rate jumped up as soon as the bodies were removed. I was determined to keep the room rate from going up.

The lobby was a discreet affair of deep mahogany paneling and Italian black marble. Now that I was standing inside, I wondered for the first time how the hell I was going to get past the desk clerk, a short dump of a kid stuffed into a gray tuxedo, without having the cops called. I wasn't ready for Dent yet.

Time was running out. I returned to the street. Major Fife smiled, ready to open the door of the blue Jaguar, and maybe earn another fifty for his initiative.

I walked right past him. Stepped off the curb. Moved back. Stared at the Inn. There was an alley between it and the building on the left. Possibly a door around back. Probably locked. Or at least alarmed. Running out of time. Come on! Oh Hell! Why hadn't I realized it? The street I was on? That building on the left. Damn! Loretta Devon's building.

I jammed the intercom buzzer. Be home. Be home. Please don't be screwing Lawson in Jersey tonight.

"Who's there?"

A *real* British voice.

"Jack Centaur. Let me in. Please!"

The oven of an elevator seemed to rise even slower than the first time. Finally, its steel door creaked open.

Backlit in the door-well of her loft, Loretta Devon stood naked under a white nightshirt. "What's the emergency?" she asked.

"I need to get onto your roof."

"What in heaven's name for?"

"Prevent a murder."

"On my roof?"

"No time to explain!"

Loretta rushed through the loft to the table where we had had our tea only a few months before. Light passing through her nightshirt showed every sensuous curve of her young body.

"This will allow you to take the lift to the roof."

I reached for the barrel-stem key Loretta held between her slender fingers. Her hand was soft. *Why would she ever let herself be touched by that turd Lawson?*

"Shall I call the police?"

"Not yet." I pulled out my cell phone. I'd given up on hearing from Maria, or from Weinberg. "Take this. Dent's speed dial is number 4. Wait an hour. Then call him."

"And tell him what?"

"Tell him he'll find the Fashion Killer next door in the Baxter's suite."

It was then when I saw the cold stare in Loretta Devon's eyes. And it scared me. I could see well this woman understood vengeance.

THIRTY-SIX

THE OVEN JOLTED UP. A cold sweat beaded my forehead.

The detail had been staring up at me all the while. Only I hadn't seen it. It was nestled there, somewhere in my accountant's subconscious. First, in the front-page photograph of Candice. Then it crept closer to the surface when I waited like a gentleman for the middle-aged woman to pass. But not until the Baxter twins took those long, slow strides up the VIP steps did the one detail rise up from the wrong column to tell me the name of the Fashion Killer.

The oven door creaked open for the last time. The black tar roof glistened under the city moon. I rushed to the ledge. A full story below I saw the terrace of the Baxter's suite. Even if I *was* twenty again, I couldn't have jumped the narrow gap between the buildings and landed a full story below without breaking my legs.

Chance is life's only certainty. Paint cans. A tarp. And leaning up against the wall of the elevator shaft—a painter's ladder.

I lowered the ladder over the ledge. Swung it gently by its extension rope until its rubber-tipped base touched softly onto the terrace. I let the top of the ladder fall back carefully against the wall of Devon's building. The first rung was down a good six, six and a half feet below the ledge.

I sat on the ledge. Swung my legs over. Took a deep breath, and turned over so my stomach was pressed down against the cold, clay shingled ridge of the ledge. I lowered my two hundred pounds, the tips of my Churches scuffing against the brick wall. My hands gripping the ledge, arms fully extended, my right foot found the first rung. Then, with both feet firmly on the rung, I took another deep breath and slid my hands from the ledge and braced them flat-palmed against the brick. My right cheek pressed against the wall, I lowered my left foot. Another rung secured, I lowered my right foot. Lowered left again. I had maybe a half-dozen more rungs to negotiate when the smooth leather sole of my shoe slipped. My right ankle twisted between rungs, I held tight to the sides of the ladder, managing somehow to keep from falling ass-backwards onto the terrace. Grimacing with pain, I endured the last few rungs down to the flat surface. It was impossible to put my full weight onto the right foot without seeing more stars than already were high above the New York skyline.

The terrace was laid rich with terracotta tiles, surrounding a bubble-domed lap-pool. A dull yellow cast from the pool's underwater lights gave the dome the look of a huge blimp resting on the roof. A night breeze rustled drapes at the far end of the terrace. Someone had left open the sliding glass door to the suite.

I slid into the shadow of the roof's perimeter wall. Reached into my back holster and pulled out the 9-millimeter. Instincts I thought long-buried beneath the scar tissue of time surfaced like the forgotten pain of an old wound.

I wanted to rush forward, but the ankle would not allow me. Instead, I limped forward, listening for movement. I heard none. Had the enemy already struck and gone, leaving the battlefield riddled with the dead? Or was the enemy just lying in ambush, waiting for me to enter the kill zone?

Remaining close to the wall, hidden from the cast of the dome's light, I came to the door. Crouching, I listened: still no sound of movement. I parted the drapes with the barrel of my weapon. Except for a slip of light entering from a crack beneath the closed door to an adjoining room, everything inside was dark. I watched for a break in the light as a sign of movement. There was none. I entered through the drapes into the dark outer room.

Dragging my bad leg, I hit a small table. It tipped and fell onto the thick carpet, its thud barely audible. I stopped. No break in the crack of light, I moved closer. Placed the fingers of my left hand easy against the closed door. The 9-millimeter steady in my right, I pushed the door slowly open. The door only had to open halfway for me to know I was too late. A naked light bulb from a shade-less lamp exposed the bodies.

Trisha and Collette were seated on a white velvet couch. Their heads leaning into each other, their long legs stretched out.

The cold sweat returned to my brow. My eyes swept the room for Maria, but the harsh glare of the naked bulb blinded me from seeing beyond the couch. I rose from my crouched position, limped three steps into the room, and once again was ambushed by my own hubris—my knees buckled, the ankle gave out. I went down, attempting to pull my weapon into my side like a linebacker trying to hang on to the football, but the floor came up too fast against my bent right elbow, jolting the killing machine loose. I made a desperate motion at grabbing my weapon back; the second blow to my head ended my quest.

I rolled onto my back. The ceiling spun, and in the blurring swirl I saw again the head of the gingerbread man. This time I kept myself from passing out. I pressed my eyelids shut, and when I opened them again, I was staring up at the silencer barrel of a .38 Special—and the face of the redheaded dyke.

"You called my cell, Jack. How can I be of help?" The voice from her mouth was Irwin Weinberg's.

Camouflaged in full view, The Fashion Killer had stalked the society jungle. The Fu Manchu moustache. The Groucho eyebrows: all as phony as Sally Down's penciled red eyebrows, blue-tinted contact lenses, and the red, butch-cut wig. And the long leather high-heeled boots to hide the bane of the transvestite: man-feet.

"Maria?" I groaned. "Where's Maria?"

"Sorry she had to tag along," Weinberg sighed. Not a remorseful sigh. Just an inconvenienced sigh. "But that's your fault, Jack. Isn't it? You used her!"

"Irwin, you better pull the trigger now. You're not going to get another chance."

"Soon. Soon." Weinberg nodded over to the Baxters. "You know it's not an act with them. They really are dumb. I said let's slip the Brooklyn Bimbo a little Ecstasy. Have a good time. 'Oh like so cool,'" Weinberg mocked the twin's high pitched voices. "I slipped them all—what do they call it in those old movies? —a Mickey, into their Red Bull."

"Do I have to stay here on the floor and listen to your little story?"

"Of course not. We're friends, Jack."

Weinberg moved back. Motioned with the .38 to a club chair near the couch. "Go ahead. Take a seat," he said. "You're going to be part of this shoot."

I rose from the floor but couldn't make a charge for Weinberg. Not with a bum ankle and the .38 pointed at my chest. So I fell back into the deep cushion of the chair, the empty holster of my weapon pressing against my back, reminding me of just what kind of schmuck I'd been not to call Dent.

Weinberg's painted lips curled into a cruel smile. "So why did you phone me?"

"To tell you my niece pointed you out as her killer."

"You've been hitting the Chivas too much."

A muscle spasmed in my neck.

"Her picture on the front page—"

"Great shot. Maybe my best...until now."

"It's a fuckup."

"What are you, another asshole critic like The Brad?"

"Bradford Lawson. That's what this is all about?"

Weinberg moved a step closer. He nodded again to the Baxters. "My first B-plan was not really to be a crime photographer, it was to be a fashion photographer. I went to Paris. The Sorbonne. After a year, my professors said there was nothing more they could teach me. I was that great! Had natural talent! So I stayed in Europe. Paris, Milan, London. Hit all the advertising agencies. All the modeling agencies. I traded off time with seventeen-year-old wannabe supermodels, doing their look-books in exchange for using the shoots to build my own look-book. And as great as my work was, I was rejected by every agency.

"So I told myself Manhattan would be better. Madison Avenue would be different. Only there really isn't a Madison Avenue anymore. Not like it was, anyway. Now the agencies are everywhere: Chelsea, The Village, Uptown, Meat Packing District. I hit them too, and it was all a big waste of time. In the fashion business great photography means nothing if you are not a twenty-something.

"But I stuck it out. Gave myself six more months. And then one day I walked in cold to Lawson Worldwide Media. Virginia Kirk was just a flunky production assistant then. She hadn't become a Lawson yet. She actually granted me ten minutes. I left her my look-book.

"She called me a week later. She was in a jam. One of her twenty-somethings had a tantrum. Walked out in the middle of a shoot. Not a big gig. But it was a chance for me to work for pay for a real agency. The shot was to be a filler piece for Spanish Vogue. Just a small picture to be stuck in a montage of promising new designers.

"I rushed over to some address Virginia gave me on the Lower Eastside. I met with three whacko designers and understood why the twenty–something ran out. But it was Fargo who was the real putz. I took the shots and got the hell out of there. I didn't even bother to email the pictures to Virginia. I printed them out at a local graphics shop, and went straight up to Lawson Worldwide.

"Virginia loved my work. Said she'd call me later. I rushed out of the office. I knew this was the break I had been waiting for. As I'm leaving I pass the big man himself. The Brad entering his fiefdom, followed by a cadre of well-dressed B-schoolers. You know how he's always bragging about the shit Business School his father bought him into. No fucking Harvard that's for sure. So there he is prancing like he's a well-hung stallion. Nodding with that pursed-lipped half-smile of his that says I'm great and you're all shit.

"Well Jack, that fat production assistant didn't call that day. And she didn't call the next! So I called her. Got her voice mail. I called her twice more, but she was still avoiding me. I left a final voice mail saying I was coming right up to her office. Within two minutes she returned my call. Says they are not going to use my pictures. She'll get me paid, but she can't go with them.

"So I pushed the bitch. You loved them! Just what you needed. What happened?

"What happened? Lawson walked through with the flunky-crew, saw my shots on her desk and announced, 'This stuff is garbage!'"

"So that was it," I said, inching forward in the chair, the front of my jacket buckling away from my chest. "Guy blows off your work and you start killing his models. You asshole. I'd take ten Brad Lawsons over a sick bastard like you."

"Jack," Weinberg moved a step closer, his eyes bulging, the .38 now pointed squarely at my head. "I dreamed of a million scenarios of how to get back at the scumbag. The same way you do when the cashier at the supermarket says something smart-ass to you and you drive home thinking of all the things you should have retorted back with and didn't. Or when the car mechanic screws you, and you want to punch him out, but you pay the bill anyway and leave. That's the way I felt. I'm not crazy!"

"No. Not you, Irwin. You're not crazy, you're a Harvard man."

"Look. I did what any smart entrepreneur would have done. I revisited my B-plan. I needed to find a niche. It was then that I came across Weegee. Age wouldn't be against me in his field. Crime Photography is wide open to anyone who gets the most sensational first picture. So I did just like Weegee did back in his time. I built a network of cops. I hung out in cop bars. Bought them drinks. Listened to them when they griped about the family not understanding their work. I listened to their bragging about their lovers. Made sure to put a couple of the cops into a few front-page shots when they called me to a crime scene. It was better than money to them, seeing their faces in the newspaper. So I was the first one to get the call whenever there was something big. Made plenty of money at it too! Long before The Fashion Killer shots."

"Your friend Detective Bark thinks you're making too much money."

"He's the only one I have to pay in cash. But he's worth it."

"That's why you call his precinct instead of 9-1-1."

"Very good, Jack."

"So if you were such a great success, why the hell did you have to get back at Lawson?"

"Funny how things happen. Two years after Lawson blew me off I'm out in drag—I've been a transvestite ever since I was twelve, dressing up in my mother's underwear. Didn't get full out until I dropped out of medical school and moved to Amsterdam for a few years. Now, there's a city for you!

"So I'm out in drag one night, sitting in the Mocha Shoppe, and this young Asian woman is bragging how Bradford Lawson's going to make her the next big supermodel. She'd just come from a $1,000-a-plate fundraiser where he had promised to make her a star.

"He was going to make this kid a star. Like the model has anything to do with it. The photographer makes the star. You ever see these anorexic mannequins before a shoot? They all live off bottled water and cigarettes. No, it's the person behind the camera who makes them the next big thing.

"I got friendly with her. Let her brag. I walked her home. Just a couple of blocks away. Said she shared the place with another model who was in Singapore on a long shoot. Wouldn't be back for weeks. Then she brags she's doing another fundraiser for the Young Metropolitans the following week. I wished her luck.

"The following week I followed her back to her place. By then I had developed a new B-plan: Laying out Lawson girls. And I'd get even more famous being the first to take the crime scene picture. And Lawson would eventually fall. Who the hell would want to be a Lawson Girl?"

"Looks like your B-plan is going to fail. Lawson's got every New Yorker rooting for him. He's put up a reward. Set up a fund for the families of the victims. He's even got his new best friend, Irwin Weinberg, to stop publishing the crime scene photographs until the heinous fiend is captured."

"That's the best part. The fool. So what if I sit in jail? New York doesn't have the death penalty. If I'm caught, I get life. And I'll sit in my jail cell laughing at Bradford Lawson. And the world will know that Irwin Weinberg is a great artist."

A moan came from somewhere in the back of the room. Behind the glare of the blinding light bulb. Maria. She was still alive!

As calm as an anesthetist, Weinberg said, "The drug is wearing off."

My eyes jutted towards the Baxter twins.

"They're not dead. None of them!" I said.

Weinberg reached into his pants pocket, pulled out an old Palm Pilot.

I leaned forward mocking, "Checking your schedule?"

With his thumb, Weinberg pushed up the stylus out of the side of the Palm Pilot. He gripped the stem with his fingers while returning the Pilot to his pocket. When his hand was in full view again, he turned the stylus point up. It was ground to the surgical sharpness of a scalpel. He smiled.

"I think your mother would say, Irwin, what a waste of your brain."

Weinberg lost his smile. "Before you die, tell me, what was wrong with the photograph of Candice? I wanted to use it for the cover of my book. In your honor: the uncle who died trying to find his niece's murderer."

"That picture on the front page, it wasn't the picture you took that morning in the bathroom when your camera flashed from behind me."

Weinberg pressed his lips.

"Someone, maybe a cop, who knows, touched the body after you took the real first picture. The picture you shoot right after you kill. The one you take right before you leave for a random phone booth and call Bark's precinct. And then you wait for Bark to call your cell phone. Maybe it was you, Irwin, who brushed against her foot before you left my niece on that cold bathroom floor. That's right, you son-of-a-bitch. Maybe it was you who slipped up. However it happened, doesn't matter. In the front-page photograph her foot is in a normal walking position, with the tip of her shoe horizontal, pointed towards the wall. When I was standing over her, staring down, her foot was extended out, the tip of the Prada pointing at the door. Pointing at you, Irwin, where you stood behind me shooting what was really the second picture you had taken that night of Candice, the one that you were never going use on the front-page."

Weinberg moved closer to me. The .38 held in his right hand and the scalpel-sharp stylus in his left.

I leaned forward an inch more in the chair. My right hand pressed against my chest, my fingertips slowly slipping inside my jacket. I must have looked like a man about to have a coronary.

Weinberg took one more step closer. Pointed the .38 straight between my eyes.

I parried Weinberg's right forearm with my left, pushing the .38 aside. A shot zipped from the silencer into the chair's deep cushion, just missing my left ear.

My right hand now reached quickly into my jacket pocket, and came out as Weinberg thrust the scalpel with his left. I catapulted up on my good right leg, my shoulder throwing off the scalpel blow. My right fist shoved the point of my Mont Blanc deep into Weinberg's jugular.

I kept pushing, extending my good leg until it was completely straight and locked at the knee.

First, Weinberg's boot heels lifted off the floor. Then the toe tips lifted up. His eyes bulging, his red wig askew, his blood dripping down my clenched fist and onto the cuff of my white shirt. I forced the pen further up until I could no longer grip it with my fist. Then I pushed the pen even further up with the heel of my palm until I felt the cracking of bone and knew my weapon had pierced through the back of the enemy's neck. I heard the gurgling of the bastard drowning in his own blood and I smiled. I had collected the debt.

EPILOGUE

B ENNY WANG ALMOST PASSED OUT when I handed him the check for $250,000. It was a little harder to get Maria to accept the remaining half of Lawson's reward. She had already fought with me over all those expensive outfits Nelka and Wayne had personally delivered to her door. As for the Fargo design I had commissioned at the gala. I called Vinny and said, 'forget about it. Keep the money, you'll be needing it now that Virginia has dumped you.' I finally convinced Maria that she had deserved every dime of the reward. That I'd only taken Lawson's money to see the humiliation on the blowhard's pucker-face when he had to give up the bucks. There was no way The Brad could spin this one. The fact that he had boasted on live television that Irwin Weinberg—The Fashion Killer!—was his "close friend." The media was having a field day. Only Tommy Convoy didn't take the road of cheap shots. But then Convoy was the lone, true journalist in the entire bunch. He wrote his last column on the subject for the families of the victims, and not for his own self-indulgence.

Michael Lawson had finally shown some backbone. He quietly announced he wanted to join his brother and serve in the military. I had called the kid. Told him not to go off to fight a war because he had lost the love of his life. It wouldn't make him a good soldier if he went around taking unnecessary chances because he felt he had nothing else to lose. *"Because you do have plenty to lose,"* I told *Michael. "And it isn't your father's money that has spotted you to a life free from the worries of paying the rent, or the payments on the Chevy, or feeding the kids, or any of that stuff that makes most people head to their cubicles every workday." No, what I told Michael he had to lose was that breath of fresh air he took in every morning. The simple walk he took down the street. The hope of a future. "All silly sounding stuff when said out loud, but not so silly when you're looking back on a life filled with self-inflicted voids."*

But Michael Lawson was young, and my words didn't matter. The kid enlisted.

I TOOK A last sip of Chivas Regal, spilled the ice cubes into the sink drain, and rinsed the glass under the running faucet. I gazed out through the kitchen window. I loved this view from Brooklyn looking over the Promenade and the moonlit ripples of the East River, to the sparkle of the Manhattan skyline—the Statue of Liberty a pastel green, downriver to my left, the Brooklyn Bridge on my right. I placed the glass upside-down in the dish rack, dried my hands with a paper towel. Tossed the towel into the plastic trash basket beneath the sink. I turned away from the window and let my eyes fall gently across the fourth-floor apartment of the brownstone. Everything was still as Sharon's parent's had left it.

The Weiner's had taken only a few personal items. They left everything else. Sharon's clothes still hung in the bedroom closet. They couldn't throw them out. They wouldn't give them away. And yet, they were afraid to take the clothes with them for fear of remembering too much.

They had forgotten a framed picture on the fireplace mantel. I had called them at their new house and Mrs. Weiner said she had left it for me. I lifted the picture. A happy family, the Weiners; Martin, Anna, Steven and their youngest, Sharon.

They moved to the West Coast a month after Sharon's funeral. "You run the place, Jackie. Your parents live rent-free. You manage it for us, collect the rents. Work hard, Jackie, make something of yourself."

If Sharon's parents hadn't left me the responsibility of the brownstone, I knew I would have run. Would have left Brooklyn forever. But I stayed. Martin and Anna both passed away. Steven became an ophthalmologist. I eventually bought the brownstone from him.

I sat the picture back on the mantel. Thought of the photograph in Loretta Devon's place. Of her father. Her mother. My accountant's mind telling me Bradford Lawson had something to do with that mess. Lawson had tried his hand at the record business back around the time the picture must have been taken. And from the look in Loretta's eyes that night I had given her my cell phone, I knew, she too, was out for vengeance. Yes, something was in the wrong column with Devon and The Brad.

Loretta had done what I asked that night. Waited the hour.

Dent had come within minutes of her call.

At the press conference, Dent had explained that when he arrived at the scene it was clear that Mr. Centaur had acted in self-defense.

Watching Dent on television I knew that the detective was thinking of his father, not Jack Centaur, when he told the press, The Fashion Killer had chosen the wrong man to mess with. A Vietnam Vet. An old fox, armed with nothing more than a ballpoint pen.

The next morning Dent came to me in the hospital. See how my broken ankle was doing. See if I needed anything.

From my hospital bed I told Dent about the 9-millimeter. Told him the truth. That I'd come packing a weapon.

"When you found it," I asked, "what did you do with it?"

"9-millimeter? Don't know anything about a 9-millimeter. Only piece we found in the suite was Weinberg's .38 Special," Dent said, then added, "Hey! What'd you do? Have the Devon girl call your partner before she called me? You afraid I might not come? How do you think it looks? I pull up and there's Andy Smoothe already standing in front of the place, heavy into conversation with some guy dressed up like a fricken Drum Major."

It was then, when, knowing no call had be made to anyone other than to Dent, that I had relaxed in the hospital bed with my hands comfortably behind my head, a faint smile hidden in the corner of my mouth, thankful Andy once again had had my back.

THE END

About The Author

MICKEY WYTE WAS BORN AND raised in Brooklyn, NY. He now resides in New Jersey with his wife and their 10-year-old boxer dog, River. River is also Mickey's writing buddy, lying quietly on the writing room carpet until biscuit-break time.

For more about Mickey Wyte please visit:
mickeywyte.com

Please follow on Twitter:
@MickeyWyte